RELIC

THE DEAN CURSE CHRONICLES

STEVEN WHIBLEY

Published by Steven Whibley Publishing
Victoria, British Columbia
www.stevenwhibley.com

Publisher: Steven Whibley
Editing: Mahak Jain; Maya Packard
Copyediting: Maya Packard, Chandler Groover
Cover Design: Pintado (rogerdespi.8229@gmail.com)
Interior Layout and Design: www.tammydesign.ca

Library and Archives Canada Cataloguing in Publication

Whibley, Steven, 1978-
       Glimpse / Steven Whibley.

(Book two of the Dean Curse chronicles)
Issued in print and electronic formats.
ISBN 978-0-9919208-5-3 (bound).--ISBN 978-0-9919208-4-6 (pbk.).--
ISBN 978-0-9919208-6-0 (pdf)

       I. Title. II. Series: Whibley, Steven, 1978- . Dean Curse
chronicles ; bk. 2.

PS8645.H46R45 2013   jC813'.6   C2013-904200-8
                                                             C2013-904201-6

For Isaiah

– Steven Whibley

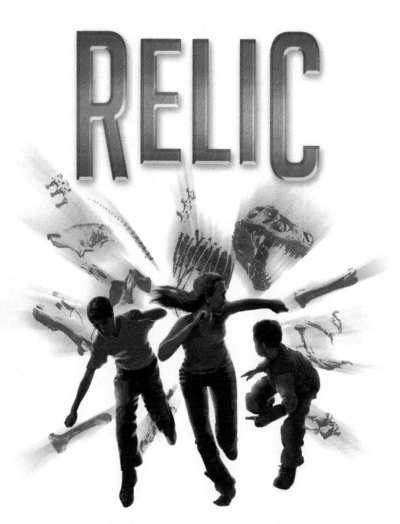

RELIC

THE DEAN CURSE CHRONICLES

STEVEN WHIBLEY

CHAPTER 1

I checked my watch. "We have sixteen minutes."

"We're in a mall," Colin said. "There are literally a million ways he could die. I mean, he could slip on someone's spilled juice box and crack his head open. Or fall down the escalator. Or maybe a chimpanzee from the pet store on the second floor will escape and—"

"I can't believe you're joking about this," Lisa said, cutting him off. "Do you realize we're talking about a man's life?" She shook her head, then peered down the mall and chewed her lip.

"I'm not joking, Lisa," Colin said. "I'm just saying that we don't have a clue how it's going to happen."

"Well, it doesn't need to be said," she snapped. "We all know what we're up against."

"Okay, okay," I said. "We can fight later. Right now we need to stay close to him."

The man, Arnold Cosler, was standing at a sunglasses kiosk less than twenty-five meters away, but we'd been following him for the past four hours—ever since he left his house at eight that morning. We were tired, we were scared, and the stress of it was totally taking its toll.

"We can't keep up with him if we stay together," Lisa said. Her eyes darted to me and the cast on my leg, then away. "I'm sorry," she said. "It's not your fault, I know that. But..." she gestured to my leg. "You're slower right now, and..." She sighed. "We just can't fail, you know?"

I nodded. "Fine. You two go ahead. I'll hang back and maybe I'll see something from a distance that might help. Just go, and keep your eyes open."

They sped up and I glanced at my cast and swore. My leg wasn't even sore anymore, and I should've had my cast off by now, but the doctors thought I needed a bit longer, just to keep me from doing anything dangerous. "Extra cast time," they'd called it. It felt like a time-out and I hadn't had one of those since I was four. It was embarrassing.

I glanced at my watch. We only had twelve more minutes. Why couldn't he just go to a park and feed ducks on his lunch break? Why'd he have to come to a mall where, like Colin said, there were literally a million ways he could die?

The vision I'd had nearly twenty-four hours before had been as freaky as every other vision I'd ever had: full of colorless, twisted shrieks of someone soon to be dead. The biggest problem we had was figuring out who Arnold Cosler was. At the time all I knew was I'd run into the man—literally—at the McDonald's a few blocks from my house about a month before.

How I'd managed to remember him was beyond me.

The biggest break was the fact that during the vision I'd kept it together enough to notice he had a dorky, car-shaped lapel pin that said, *Ask me about our lease options*. If I hadn't seen that button I don't know if we would have ever found him. But as it was, the third car dealership we went to had salesman Arnold Cosler's picture on the wall.

And now here we were, about to either save him or watch him die.

I hobbled around a collection of sofas set up in the middle of the concourse and stepped up beside a Bob the Builder quarter ride. Across the concourse Mr. Cosler handed his credit card to the salesgirl manning the sunglasses kiosk. I took a second to glance around the area, hoping I'd spot something that might give me a clue of what was to come.

There was a shoe store with a bunch of balloons out front—some kind of grand reopening or something. An elderly man was asleep in one of those two-dollar massage chairs, and another man wearing a white shirt and white pants—which had to be a uniform of some kind—was reading a newspaper on one of the benches. There were a few people milling around, but really it was only noon on a weekday. The mall was mostly empty.

I peered overhead at the ceiling three stories above and wondered if one of the glass panels might detach itself and smash into him, but that seemed really unlikely since Lisa and Colin were practically on top of him, and I hadn't had any visions of their deaths.

I glanced back at my watch. Eight minutes. Mr. Cosler had wandered away from the sunglasses kiosk and had stopped at a place selling funnel cakes.

That's when I heard the scream.

I whirled around and glanced to the second story where the scream had come from. Pretty much right above Mr. Cosler, a toddler in a pink dress was having a Category 4 temper tantrum. From my vantage point it wasn't easy to see, but it seemed like she was stomping and shouting and at one point she even threw a handful of something that hit her frazzled father and rained down over the balcony.

Somehow everyone heard the screams, but no one seemed to notice the tiny pellets she'd thrown, probably raisins or Cheerios or some other toddler food.

Focus! I turned back to Mr. Cosler. He was still at the funnel cake shop, waiting for his order. Lisa and Colin looked at me expectantly and I shrugged. My watch was counting down the last couple minutes and I didn't have a clue what was going to happen.

The funnel cake guy pulled Mr. Cosler's snack from the deep fryer and dusted it in whatever flavor he'd ordered and handed it over. Mr. Cosler nodded to the man, took a bite, and continued wandering through the mall.

All I could come up with was he'd choke to death. Nothing else made sense. But it was a funnel cake. Who choked on a funnel cake?

I crutched my way along the wall, coming up along the same path Mr. Cosler had taken. As I passed the funnel cake shop, something crunched under my foot and I glanced down. M&Ms, peanuts, and raisins dotted the floor. Clearly the little girl above had picked trail mix as her weapon of choice.

I kept moving.

Cosler had taken a few bites of his funnel cake, and as he paced down the concourse, the light shining through the glass windows overhead glinted off his wrist. At first I thought it was his watch, but then I spotted a watch on his other wrist, which meant the first one was...a bracelet?

The only guy I knew who wore a bracelet was Reggie Sung, a kid in my grade who was about as tough as a flower petal. His bracelet was a Medic Alert; we used to joke that he was allergic to bravery.

I jerked back and stared through the glass of the funnel cake shop and saw some of the trail mix beside the deep fryer. Some of it must've fallen into the fryer too. *And what is the main ingredient in trail mix?* a voice in my head asked.

That was it! I waved to Lisa and Colin. Colin looked over at me and I pointed at Mr. Cosler, then at my wrist. "He's allergic to nuts," I shouted.

"What?" Colin shouted back.

The color faded and the world became shades of gray: it was time to act. We had to do something now; our window of opportunity wasn't going to last long.

"Peanuts!" I practically screamed as I half hobbled, half ran. "He's allergic to peanuts!"

Colin's eyes widened and he spun around. Mr. Cosler was hunched over, coughing. His funnel cake, half-eaten, was on the floor.

I couldn't use my crutches and call 9-1-1, so I shouted, "Somebody call an ambulance!"

Lisa was at the man's side in a flash, and Colin a second later, just in time to have Mr. Cosler fall against him and the two of them hit the floor. When I arrived a few seconds after, the man had pushed himself to his knees and was trying to get something out of his coat. His wheezing had become a high-pitched squeal and his eyes were so wide I thought they might burst.

"Is he choking?" Lisa shouted in a panic.

"Nuts," I said. "He's allergic to nuts."

Mr. Cosler finally jerked something out of his coat pocket, a small cylinder the size of a large marker. I recognized it—an EpiPen, medicine to stop an allergic reaction. He was trying to do something to it, pull off the lid, maybe, it wasn't clear.

"Let me help you," Lisa said. She lunged for the medicine and knocked it out of the man's hand and sent it skittering across the floor. The man tried to grab for it, but when he missed he crumpled fully to the floor and stopped moving. Lisa let out a sound like a wounded animal and dove for the EpiPen. She grabbed it, spun back, and in one movement yanked the cap off and slammed the end of it into the man's leg and held it there, gasping and looking around frantically.

Colin was shaking the man's shoulders, shouting at him to wake up.

"Outta the way," a female voice shouted. It was a mall security guard. She rushed in through the small crowd that had formed around us, and shouldered Colin out of the way as she knelt beside Mr. Cosler. Another officer arrived a second later and pushed the crowd back while he held a cell phone to his ear, giving directions to where we were to whoever was on the other end.

"Allergy," I said, practically shouting. "He's allergic to peanuts." I pointed at his wrist and even though it had been a hunch, sure enough, it was a Medic Alert bracelet.

Color seeped back into my black and white world as the female guard started CPR.

"We were too late," Lisa said beside me. She gripped

my arm. Her hands trembled. "If I hadn't made him drop his medicine..."

"He's not dead," Colin said.

As if to prove his point, Mr. Cosler suddenly sucked in a deep breath and began coughing.

Lisa's head dropped and she let out a monumental sigh. Colin looked up at the ceiling and started laughing. Some of the people standing by started to clap. I just stared at the scene and shook my head. That was way too close. *Way* too close.

Something to my right caught my eye, and I turned just in time to see the man in white I'd noticed earlier turn and stroll away. He glanced over his shoulder once before he rounded a corner and we made eye contact. He smirked and gave me an approving nod, then stepped out of sight.

"Can we get out of here?" Lisa whispered.

I nudged Colin and gestured to the exit and the three of us slipped away.

CHAPTER 2

Colin whooped when we got outside, and I was filled with such a wave of relief that if I hadn't had crutches, I might have needed to sit down. I hadn't had a vision since Becky, my sister, and I'd been terrified something would go wrong. But it hadn't. Everything had gone exactly right. I turned to Lisa and she smiled, but not a natural smile—it was forced and looked sort of painful.

"Are you okay?" I asked.

"Why wouldn't she be okay?" Colin asked. "We just saved a guy." He pointed at Lisa. "*You* just saved that guy." He laughed. "That was practically ninja-like, the way you dove and grabbed that EpiPen and slammed it into his thigh." He jumped around, acting out Lisa's movements. "How are you not on cloud nine right now?"

"You did save him," I said.

She shook her head. "I nearly killed him. I knocked the pen right out of his hand."

"Lisa," Colin said, "he was going to die. He would have died if you hadn't jabbed him when you did. He's alive because of you." He turned and looked at me. "And you

17

too. How the heck did you know about his peanut allergy?"

I quickly recounted what happened with the screaming kid, and how I'd spotted the bracelet and assumed it was a Medic Alert bracelet.

"That's quick thinking," Colin said.

"It was luck," Lisa said. "Dumb, stupid luck." She blew out a frustrated breath. "What is taking the Society so long, anyway? I mean they said they'd be in touch, so where are they?"

She looked at me as if I had an answer. I shrugged and was about to remind her that the *Congregatio de Sacrificio* — the society I was now a part of, thanks to my visions — hadn't reached out since they left me a note over six weeks ago. But before I could say anything, my phone vibrated with a text message and I checked the screen... and groaned.

"What?" Colin asked.

I replied to the text and then looked up at my friends. "I have to meet my mom and my sister."

"Oh, right, I forgot about your little playdate with your sister," Colin said.

"I kind of think it's sweet," Lisa said.

"It's not sweet," I said. "It's weird and it violates the laws of sibling interaction."

Ever since I'd "accidentally" jumped in front of a moving vehicle to save her life, my parents had been on a big push to make Becky and me better friends. Step one in their little plan was for me to be more encouraging of her hobbies—which, by anyone's standards, were freaking weird. Mostly she collected stuff. But not normal stuff like stamps or coins or bottlecaps. A few weeks back she was collecting insects. My parents were still making me pay for stabbing one of her spiders with a fork.

"The laws of sibling interaction?" Lisa asked.

I nodded. "And they shouldn't be messed with."

"What are you guys doing today?" Colin asked. "Chocolate sundaes at the beach? Hopscotch in the park?"

Lisa laughed at that one, which made me smile. It seemed she didn't laugh these days nearly as much as she used to.

"Museum," I said. "Apparently they have an exhibit Becky's interested in."

"Sounds boring," Colin said.

"It will be."

My mom was an art history professor and the museum had a whole floor of paintings she'd helped curate several years before. I couldn't count how many times she'd dragged me there when I was younger. "You guys should come."

Colin laughed like that was the funniest thing he'd ever heard.

"I'll come," Lisa said. "I'm kind of in the mood for

boring after what we just did."

"Thanks, Lisa," I said.

Colin stopped laughing and groaned. "Fine. I'll come." We started walking around the perimeter of the mall and Colin asked, "What's your sister collecting that would be on display at a museum, anyway?"

Now it was my turn to groan. "You wouldn't believe me if I told you."

"Sounds mysterious," Lisa said.

"Trust me," I said, "it's the least mysterious collection you've ever seen."

CHAPTER 3

When we got into the car, Colin asked to see Becky's collection. She smiled and handed the box back into the back seat. I leaned away from it as Colin lifted the lid.

"It looks like rocks," Colin said.

"It's coprolite," Becky said from the front seat. "They're fossils, and pretty valuable."

I rolled my eyes. "I doubt that."

"They are!" Becky snapped. "The one at the museum is from a *Tyrannosaurus rex*." She looked over her shoulder from the front seat and sneered at me. "That's a dinosaur."

"You don't say," I muttered.

"Okay, you two," my mom said. "I don't want you guys to argue. Besides, Becky is right: if they are coprolite, they can be quite valuable."

"They're fossils?" Colin said. He reached in and picked up one of the pieces and held it up to his face. "Fossils of what?"

I started to laugh.

"It's fossilized excrement," Becky said.

Lisa was seated between Colin and me and she practically crushed me against the door trying to lean away from him and the box.

"Extra-what?" Colin asked.

"Ex-cre-ment," Becky said.

Colin blinked and then turned and looked at me.

"Turd," I said, laughing. "You're holding animal crap right now."

The coprolite dropped from his hand and he just sat there staring into the box shaking his head. "You're collecting animal turds?" His face twisted and he turned back to me.

Lisa and I burst out laughing. Even my mom laughed. Becky didn't find it very funny and reached into the back seat and grabbed the box back.

"Wait," Colin said. "They have a giant piece of dinosaur crap at the museum? On display?"

"Along with a T. rex skeleton," my mom said.

Colin dusted his hands off and then shrugged. "Actually, that sounds pretty cool." Then he whispered, "But your sister's still mega weird."

"Trust me, I know." An itch started under my cast. I tried to reach my finger down the side to scratch it. The worst part about casts is the itching. Dry spaghetti was the best thing to use for scratching, but it always broke. When the cast finally came off in a few days, I wondered how much broken spaghetti would be in there and what the doctor would say when he saw it.

I looked up when my sister gasped.

"You think they're all here for the coprolite exhibit?" she said.

A police officer leaning against his cruiser blocked most of my view, but there seemed to be a crowd gathered just beyond the officer, near the entrance. Plus, news vans from at least three different stations were parked along the street.

"Maybe," my mom said excitedly. "Or maybe they got a new art exhibit. That would be fun." She turned to face us in the back seat. "Don't you guys think so?"

"Oh, yeah, goody," I mocked.

I wasn't sure what to expect when my mom parked and we walked around the corner and headed for the entrance. I wouldn't have been too surprised to see TV reporters interviewing the museum curator. I was even ready to see a few photographers snapping pictures of a giant turd, but all five of us stopped dead in our tracks as soon as we reached the front of the building.

A dozen or so people stood just off to the side of the main doors, moving together in a tight circle and chanting, "Give it back. Give it back. Give it back." Others held signs with slogans like, "Buddha is not for display," and "Overton Supports Thieves." There were other signs too, but they were covered with seemingly random squiggles and dots, almost like a painted snake had slithered across the cardboard. I wasn't sure what the language was, but it wasn't English.

The most interesting thing, though, were the four Asian men standing near the main entrance. They all wore identical orange robes that exposed one shoulder and hung to their ankles. They had shaved heads. Three of the men were withered and wrinkled and looked so old they should probably have been on display in the museum themselves, but the fourth guy was young enough to pass as my older brother—if I had a bald Asian brother who liked robes. He kept his head down, and it took a moment, but I realized he had a cell phone and seemed to be texting someone.

"Are those monks?" Lisa asked.

"They look like monks," Colin said. "Except for that young one. Are monks supposed to have cell phones? And can monks be *that* young?"

"Yes, Colin, they can." My mom inched us toward the short line of normal-looking folks at the entrance. "I don't think this has anything to do with the coprolite exhibit, Becky," my mom added.

One of the protestors, a middle-aged woman with tight curly hair and a "Free Tibet" t-shirt, broke away from the group and rushed us as we got in line. "Don't you care that you're supporting thievery?"

Becky pressed tighter into my mom's side as the woman first sneered at us and then pointed a stern finger at my mom. "They're displaying stolen artifacts." She gestured to the monks. "These monks came all the way from Cambodia to get them back."

A couple of news crews rushed in and pointed their cameras and bright lights at us. My mom cleared her throat. "If there's something in the museum that was stolen, you should report it. There are better ways than trying to intimidate people."

"Report it?" The protestor laughed. "Who should we report it to? Cambodian authorities don't care, and the curator doesn't care. All they care about is making money and drawing a crowd." She scowled at the camera crew and then back at my mom. "Which is exactly what you're helping them do. You make me sick." She turned to the camera. "Imagine a woman bringing her kids to see a stolen head."

"Stolen head?" Colin's eyes widened to the size of Roman shields, and a smile tore his face in half. "As in an actual human head?" He laughed. "I thought we were here to see a giant turd. This is way better than I expected."

The protestor blinked. "A giant what?"

Colin looked up at the camera. "Can I say *turd* on TV?" The cameraman smiled and gave Colin a thumbs-up.

Museum security stepped up and blocked the crazy

lady from getting closer to the entrance. She grumbled, raised a fist over her head, and then returned to her group and resumed chanting, "Give it back. Give it back."

We stepped inside. A man in a dark suit stood just inside the door. "Good morning, ma'am," he said to my mom. "My name is Jonathan Overton. I'm the curator of the museum. I just wanted to extend my apologies for any discomfort caused by the protestors." He pursed his lips and blew a breath through his nose. I imagined he'd been giving the same apology to everyone who'd come in. Then he seemed to give my mom a second look. "Professor Curse?"

She extended her hand. "I'm sorry, Mr. Overton, do we know each other?"

"No, no, but my predecessor mentioned you had a lot of input on our art exhibit, and I was at your lecture on Caravaggio this past spring. Riveting."

My mom's grin widened. "Why, thank you. I was trying to introduce the..."

I stopped paying attention to the conversation and glanced at my friends. The three of us slipped away—or in my case, crutched away. Becky did too, but she went the opposite direction.

"Let's go find that head," Colin said.

A map situated in the middle of the foyer showed that each floor of the museum was shaped like a giant U.

"Second floor is artwork," Lisa said, muttering mostly

to herself as she read the map. "Here." She tapped a section marked in red. "New exhibits and items on loan. I bet the head's here. First floor."

She pointed to the right. "That way."

CHAPTER 4

The three of us made our way through the Native American exhibit and past the display of medieval weaponry. Colin stole one of my crutches and had a mock sword fight with a knight on display. He only stopped when he noticed the models of early man and jumped the ropes. He hunched over, situating himself among a trio of cavemen roasting something over a fake fire.

"Aw, that's sweet," Lisa said. "Colin's found his birth family."

"Don't listen to her, Dad," Colin said, speaking to the wax caveman to his right. "She's just jealous."

We laughed and Colin stood up and took a step but his foot clipped one of the logs in the display and he stumbled backwards through some fake foliage and smack into the back wall, then disappeared.

"Colin?"

"A little help," he said, groaning.

Lisa and I exchanged glances and I gestured to my leg. "I can't climb over all that."

Lisa sighed and glanced down the hallway. Museum

security must've been mostly outside because there weren't any guards in sight. She sighed again and quickly stepped over the barrier, pushing aside the fake bushes to reveal a door. She disappeared through it and emerged a second later, pulling Colin by the wrist.

"That hurt," Colin said, once he was back on the correct side of the display.

"Serves you right," Lisa said. "You're just lucky no one saw you."

"Where did you disappear to?" I asked.

"A garage or a loading bay of some kind," Lisa said as we started walking again. "There was a door a truck could fit through, and the room had loads of boxes and crates."

Near the end of the corridor, the hall widened into a large circular atrium, where people on the second and third floors could look down at the exhibit below. A humongous skeleton of a *Tyrannosaurus rex* stood directly in front of us. It must've been nearly twenty feet tall and forty feet long. Its head—about the size of a small car— leaned out over half the atrium, and its mouth, filled with teeth that looked bigger than my leg, opened threateningly to the people on the second floor. The colossal beast stood on a large platform covered in dirt and thick plastic bushes and large ferns that I guess were supposed to resemble its natural habitat.

The museum had had dinosaur exhibits in the past,

but usually the dinosaurs were small, like the size of a truck. This was bigger than anything I'd ever seen. "Hard to believe they were so big," I said.

As if the skeleton were made out of some giant kid magnet, the three of us gravitated toward it until we were at the velvet rope barrier.

"I have to touch it," Colin said.

Lisa shook her head. "No, you don't. This isn't like messing with mannequins dressed like cavemen. I'm sure there are real fossils in there. You could get in loads of trouble."

"Oh, c'mon, Lisa. I could duck behind some of those bushes and they'd never see me. Besides, if they didn't want people going across, they'd have put up something more threatening than velvet ropes."

"Like razor wire and a Rottweiler, perhaps?" The voice came from over our shoulders, and the three of us spun around. The security guard was a sinewy older man with graying hair. He had a name badge on his chest that said FISHER. He wore a tired expression and tapped the end of his oversized flashlight into his hand like it was a baton, seemingly prepared to bash us with it if we dared to inch too close to the dinosaur. "Just look," he said. "Don't touch."

"Yeah," I said, "we weren't going to touch."

"Sure you weren't."

"We weren't," Lisa said, backing me up.

"Fine." The guard straightened up and looked at Colin. "You weren't going to, either, I bet."

"No, I was probably going to touch it." Colin smiled and looked back at the dinosaur and then muttered under his breath, "I'll have to wait 'til you leave, I guess."

"What was that?" the guard asked.

Colin turned back. "Erm, nothing. How is this dinosaur standing up? I don't see any wires."

"They're replica bones," the guard said. "They're fastened together and then balanced the way a real T. rex would have been balanced."

"So I could just give it a shove and it would topple over?" Colin asked.

"Hardly," the guard answered. "It's bolted to the platform and there is metal running through most of the pieces, so unless you have a crowbar to smash the legs completely, I'd say you're not going to have much luck."

Colin tapped his chin. "A crowbar, eh?"

The guard drew a deep breath and exhaled through his nose, then turned and marched off.

"He was friendly," Colin said.

"Bobby, don't touch that!"

We turned toward the scolding voice—on the opposite side of the T. rex and through the skeleton, and saw a woman holding a porky little kid in her arms.

"But, Mo-om!"

"No buts, Bobby. You don't touch poop. I don't care how old it is. Let's go look at something else. Something clean."

We stepped around the T. rex display and saw what Becky had been making such a fuss about. On a bone-white platform just a couple of meters to the right of the dinosaur was a dark gray blob, about two feet long and about half a foot across, which didn't seem large considering how big the dinosaur was. It looked like a giant golf tee dipped in concrete.

Becky was already there, snapping pictures and jotting down who-knows-what in her little notebook. She turned away and pretended she didn't know us when we walked up.

"I thought it would be bigger," Colin said.

Lisa pointed to the sign beside the display. "It's five kilograms. That's pretty big."

"I guess so." Colin turned back to the dinosaur. "But look how big he is. His turd should be like the size of a truck or something."

"Maybe it was the size of a truck," Lisa said. "But that's all that managed to last over the past million years or so." She gave her head a shake. "Are we really discussing this?"

Colin's eyes widened and he nodded down the atrium a bit farther. "There's the head."

"And one of the monks," Lisa said.

The head was on a podium, like the kind the principal speaks behind during assemblies, and covered in a glass box. And sure enough, one of the monks—the young one—was standing beside the head with his arms crossed over his chest, looking incredibly unfriendly.

"What are we waiting for?" Colin said.

Lisa shook her head and grabbed Colin's arm to hold him back as a couple wandered close to the monk and the severed head. The monk must've said something because both people suddenly took a step back, and the woman looked positively insulted. They shook their heads disapprovingly at the monk and abruptly walked away.

"I don't think he's there to answer questions," Lisa said. "Maybe we should just keep our distance."

Colin shook out of Lisa's grip. "No way. When will I ever have a chance to see a severed head again? Probably never." He tilted his head toward another exhibit near the monk. "We'll wander that way and casually make our way over."

We did just that—even stopping at a display called the Rube Goldberg machine—a huge pinball-type contraption—and playing with it for a few minutes, just to make sure we didn't seem overly interested in the head.

When we finally reached the Cambodian head display, we all responded with the same unimpressed expression: "Oh."

I think we were all expecting something different.

I thought it was going to be an actual severed human head. I thought it would be like the movies, that maybe the guy's tongue would be hanging out the side of his mouth or maybe his eyes would be rolled back in his head. But no, it was nothing like that.

There were three podiums. The first held a stone hand that looked like it should be holding something. The second, the one in the middle, had a bare foot, also carved from stone. And on the third podium was the severed head. It was about twice the size of a normal head and had a round face and a pleasant expression, as if the man hadn't been at all upset about being separated from his body. A small white card beneath it read: *Sandstone Buddha Head, Cambodia, 12th Century.*

"That's it?" Colin asked. "That's what all the protesters are shouting about? I thought it was supposed to be a real head."

"I thought it would be creepier," Lisa said.

I nodded. "Yeah, I didn't expect him to look so happy."

The monk stepped forward, his hands hidden beneath the folds of his robe. "Are you done?" He didn't wait for us to respond before adding, "Good. Get lost."

Lisa looked about as shocked as I felt. "W—What?" she asked.

"You heard me." He spoke with an English accent, which was completely at odds with what the protestors had said. Unless my geography was really wrong, Cambodia wasn't at all near England.

"First of all, baldy," Colin said, "this is a public place, and we'll stay if we want. And second, if you have a problem with people looking at your village's statues, maybe you should hire a lawyer."

The monk lowered his chin and muttered something that sounded like, "I'm done dealing with lawyers." Then he took an aggressive step forward. Now, Colin may be the movie buff in our little group, but I'd seen enough to know that monks can be trained fighters. I tried to step back out of striking distance, but my stupid leg didn't move as quick as my mind told it to, and I staggered. My arms flailed, my crutches clattered to the tiled floor, and I tipped backward.

This is going to hurt.

I clenched my eyes shut, preparing for the impact, only to feel someone grab me. I tried to spin around and regain my balance but only managed a half turn before my elbow struck something that I might have seen if my eyes weren't still closed. The impact felt softer than it should've, and when I opened my eyes, all I could see was orange.

I groaned, then blinked as a bright light flashed to my right. *I must've hit my head on the tiles*, I thought, still blinking. It took me a moment to realize that the orange mass I was lying on was really the monk. No sooner did that realization strike than Colin and Lisa were beside me, hauling me to my feet.

"Did he push you... or help you?" Lisa asked. "It happened so fast I didn't see."

"I think he pushed him," Colin said.

The monk sat up and rubbed a red mark on the side of his head. I figured it was probably from my elbow. There was another flash, this time on my left. A man, crouched low, snapped one picture after another. Then something else caught my eye. Another man. He was standing just behind a book display, and I only caught a glimpse of his face. It was just a flash before he pulled back into the shadows. But one glimpse was all I needed. I knew where I'd seen him before.

At the mall. He wasn't wearing his uniform anymore, but it was still him—the man in white.

CHAPTER 5

Colin hauled me to my feet and handed me one of my crutches. I grabbed his shoulder both for support and so he'd know that what I was about to say was serious. "He's here."

Colin blinked and then focused on my eyes. "What? Who?"

"The man in white."

Colin blinked again and I remembered I hadn't told them about him.

"A guy from the mall—I think he might be following us." I looked over Colin's shoulder and spotted the man standing beside the Rube Goldberg pinball machine. "There," I said. I turned and pointed. "We need to find out who he is."

"Probably a reporter," Colin said with a grin. "Probably wants an interview."

"That would be bad," I said, reminding him that we'd agreed to keep a low profile so that we wouldn't draw any attention to the Society. "We don't need them having second thoughts about letting us join."

The monk staggered to his feet and muttered

something under his breath that I'm pretty sure wasn't English. I turned to face him as Lisa stepped beside him and steadied him.

"I'm sorry about hitting you," I said. "It was an accident."

The monk glowered and rubbed his temple. "Sure it was."

I glanced back over my shoulder as the mystery man turned and casually made his way down the corridor toward the exit. "There," I said. "There he is, in the blue windbreaker." I looked expectantly at Colin and Lisa. Neither of them moved. "I can't follow him," I said, gesturing to my leg. "C'mon, at least get his license plate number."

Lisa nodded and bolted after the man.

"You can't let her go alone," I said.

"I can't promise I won't give an interview," Colin said with a grin before he spun around sharply and sprinted away. I hadn't moved my hand off Colin's shoulder quick enough and his momentum spun me like a top. I staggered back into the monk as he was fixing his robes; this time when we hit the ground, I heard something crunch.

I tried to get up, but was tangled in the monk's robe, and he heaved on it, trying to pull the edge out from under me. I rolled once and then used my crutch to pull myself back to my feet. The crowd grew, and the camera flashes really started going nuts.

"I'm so sorry." I reached out to help the monk to his

feet only to stop short as a harsh voice shouted over my shoulder. The yell was followed by heavy footfalls.

I knew it was a guard, but before I could turn and explain, he tackled me. Bolts of pain coursed through my body as we hit the floor and rolled over each other. Twice. When the world stopped spinning, I was on my back, gazing dumbly through the atrium's glass ceiling, wondering where all the little stars had come from.

Rough hands hauled me to my feet and dragged me back to the severed head display, where the monk was being helped to his feet by another security guard.

"W—What's going on?" I choked out. I tried to shrug off the guards' hands, but they weren't having it. Their grip tightened. "Hey, let me go," I said. "I didn't do anything."

The guard on my right grunted. "That's not what it looked like to me."

"Pounding on a monk," the other guard muttered. "Pathetic."

The monk rubbed the side of his head and glared at me.

"Pounding on the monk?" I was incredulous. "I wasn't trying to hit you."

I remembered that Lisa and Colin had gone after the mystery man, and jerked my head around, scanning the spectators. I spotted them squeezing through the crowd, coming back to me. Lisa looked me square in the eyes and shook her head, indicating she and Colin hadn't caught up with him. Colin, on the other hand, was inching toward me, his gaze fixed on my leg. I glanced down and realized there was a trail of plaster chunks leading from where I'd been tackled to where I stood. At least a third of my cast was gone, crushed by the guard and reduced to shards. It looked as though my leg had been mauled by a pack of hyenas.

Colin nodded. "You really need to work on what *low profile* means."

"It was an accident," I muttered. Not that it did any good. One of the guards thrust my crutches at me and gestured down the hall. "C'mon, let's go."

CHAPTER 6

My mom spoke to Mr. Overton for nearly twenty minutes, at least ten of which were spent in the security office watching surveillance footage. I was brought in to watch it too, and I had to admit, it did look like I was pummeling the poor guy. But really it was just awkward movements because of my stupid cast.

They sent me back out into the waiting area, and when Mom came back, she handed me my crutches and led us to the car without speaking. The number of protestors had doubled, but they either didn't notice us as we left or they saw the murderous expression on my mom's face and decided not to chance a confrontation.

The young monk was around the side of the building, his head hanging as the three ancient monks talked to him with stern expressions. He glowered at me when we rounded the corner but turned away when one of the elderly monks nudged his arm.

I didn't even try to fight Becky for the front seat. She smirked but, to her credit, didn't utter a word. She was a brat, but not a stupid brat. She knew what my mom's cold expression meant: don't speak. My mom clearly had something to say, and snark from anyone in the car simply wouldn't be tolerated until she was done. When the doors were closed, Mom drew a series of shallow breaths and turned to face me.

"Mom, I just wanted—"

She held up her finger, cutting me off. "Uh-uh," she said. "Not a word." Long seconds passed before she seemed to relax a bit. "Dean," she said finally, "that was unacceptable."

"It was an accident."

"I saw the footage," she said. "You three seemed to antagonize that poor boy, and then... well, you saw it, Dean. You elbowed him in the head and practically tackled him."

"You did?" Colin asked. He sounded more impressed than surprised, and I was pretty sure that if my mom hadn't been looking, he'd have raised his hand for a high five.

Lisa gave me a squinty-faced *You did that?* look, and I just shook my head.

"It was an accident!" I turned back to my mom. "I told you that already."

"Didn't look very accidental from where I was sitting," she said. "Lucky for you, Mr. Overton didn't seem to think it was on purpose. But to me, it looked like you were really going after him." She took a breath and forced it out through her nose. "He's a kid too, Dean. He's probably not much older than you are."

"We didn't antagonize him," Lisa said hesitantly. "We really didn't. We were just looking at the display and he got really upset about it."

My mom turned in her seat to face us. "I was just talking to some people about this, and you kids need to understand something. Those monks believe that relic has been stolen. They've been protesting its display for a very long time. That head is on loan from a museum in Amsterdam. Those monks followed it all the way here, and they'll follow it to the next place too. Imagine if there was something you respected and revered so much that you'd follow it around the world hoping that people would return it to you. Now imagine people mocking it. Or gawking at it disrespectfully. How do you think you'd feel?"

"I think I get it," Becky said. "I like coprolite, and Dean makes fun of me for it. He's pretty much made fun of all of my collections."

Colin snorted and tried to cover it up as a cough.

"Not exactly the same thing, dear," Mom said, "but you're on the right track." She turned back to us. "Now you and that monk aren't allowed back in the museum for the rest of the summer. In fact, Mr. Overton's talking about banning all four of the monks just to make sure nothing like this happens again."

It took all my willpower not to laugh. *Oh, no. What am*

I going to do with myself if I can' t go to the museum?

My mom sighed and turned in her seat and started the car. "Put yourself in his shoes, Dean."

"Was he wearing shoes?" Colin whispered.

"I can't believe you punched a monk," Becky said. "Who punches a monk?"

"I didn't punch him."

"Oh, right. Okay, who elbows a monk in the head and then tackles them to the floor? Plus, who gets kicked out of a museum?" She tsked. "It's a museum, for Pete's sake. Doesn't exactly attract the crazies."

"Tell that to that mob of protestors," Colin said. "They seemed plenty crazy."

"Takes one to know one," Becky muttered.

Lisa laughed, then glanced at my mom and stopped.

"All right, you guys, that's enough." My mom sighed. "Now we have to go to the hospital to get that cast—or what remains of it—taken care of. I'll let *you* tell the doctor what happened."

Becky turned in her seat and smirked. "Monk Puncher. That's your new name. Monk Puncher Curse."

"Hmm, Monk Puncher Curse," Colin mused. "Actually, that has a bit of a ring to it. Sort of sounds like a boxer." He smiled. "You should keep it."

I sighed. "Oh, shut up, Colin."

Hospitals always seem to have one of those smells that hit you in the face like a brick and overwhelm your senses so that one second you're ready to puke, and the next you're fine. I think the people who run hospitals create that smell on purpose just to distract you from the pain that brought you there in the first place.

I breathed through my mouth while I waited to see the doctor.

The only good thing about all this was finally I'd be getting my cast off. Not that it was really on at the moment. Maybe seventy-five percent was still intact, and if I'd had a pair of garden shears, it would have been off in a flash. When I suggested that to my mom in an attempt to lighten her dark mood she gave me a silent withering look.

Becky, though, had insisted on staying in the car to go over her coprolite notes and scroll through her museum pictures, which I figured was one of those little silver lining moments that greeting cards always talk about.

"Take a seat," Mom said, pointing to the waiting area. "I'll go fill out the paperwork."

Every other time I'd been in the hospital, the waiting room had been packed or very nearly packed. This time, though, there were only three other people. Two of them were asleep, and the third was reading a magazine in the corner. We took seats well away from everyone else and discussed the situation.

"The guy you saw," Lisa asked, "are you sure he was at the mall?"

"A hundred percent," I said. "He had on white pants and a white button-up shirt."

"Like an ice cream man?" Lisa asked.

"Actually, yeah," I said. "Exactly like an ice cream man."

"We saw an ice cream truck driving away from the museum," Colin said.

"Do you think," Lisa began hesitantly, "that he's from the Society?"

"An ice cream man?" Colin said. "No way."

I looked at Lisa. "I don't know. I guess it could be a coincidence."

A janitor wearing a faded blue hat and dark coveralls entered the room and set up CAUTION signs around where we were sitting. He pulled a dry mop from his yellow cart and started making his way down the aisle we were in. When he was a couple paces away, he pulled out a scraper and knelt. "Your leg looks like it's in rough shape," the janitor said. He kept his head down so I couldn't see his face, but his voice sounded like he was smiling. "I hope you're okay."

"I'll be fine, thank you," I said. "I'm, um, getting it, or

the rest of it, off today."

"That's good," he said. "Fighting monks will be a lot easier when you're not in a cast."

"I don't expect that to happen again. Wait—how did you know about the museum?"

The janitor looked up and smiled. "The name's Astley, Archer Astley." He looked a bit different—darker hair, no white clothes—but there was no mistaking his face.

Lisa gasped. "You're the guy Dean saw at the mall. The ice cream man."

CHAPTER 7

Colin gave a frightened yelp, grabbed a magazine, and lightning-fast, rolled it into a tube and held it out like a dagger. "Who are you, and why are you following us?" He inched forward, his arm extended, until he positioned himself bravely between us and the ice cream man—or janitor, I supposed.

With the man on his knees, it actually seemed as though Colin and his rolled-up magazine had the upper hand.

The man smiled and sat back on his heels. "Wow, that's a first." He turned to me. "You have some good friends, Dean. I'm so glad to see that." His grin widened when he turned back to Colin. "You three shouldn't be surprised to see me. I did send Dean a card telling him I'd be in touch."

Lisa inhaled sharply and looked at Colin and then back at Archer. "You're from the..."—she dropped her voice to a whisper—"Society?"

The man nodded and gave a slight bow. "At your service."

Colin slapped his paper weapon into his palm. "I knew it!" He pointed at me and then Lisa. "I told you they'd

48

be in touch soon, didn't I?" He laughed again and then he stopped and his eyebrows nearly touched each other as he turned back to Archer. "Wait, you're from the Society and what, you sell ice cream and clean hospitals on the side? That doesn't sound right."

"Not really," Archer said. "This..."—he nodded at us— "you three, are a rather unique case for us. How does an adult approach a couple kids and invite them into a millennia-old society? We have pretty strict rules about who knows about us, but those rules kind of fly out the window when we're talking about kids." He smiled. "Frankly, we needed to watch you guys. We needed to figure out who you were going to tell and how committed you are to our cause."

"Then you saw us today?" Colin asked.

Archer nodded. "Amazing job, guys. Your teamwork was incredible." He smiled at me. "Good job spotting the nuts. I'm sure I would've missed that."

Colin dropped into one of the seats and blew out a breath. "So you're the contact."

"I'm the contact," Archer said.

"This is crazy," Colin added. "I feel like I'm in a movie." He glanced over his shoulder and then leaned forward so his face was almost at the same height as Archer's. "Are there secret handshakes we need to learn?"

"Huh?" Archer shook his head. "No. No secret handshakes, Colin." He glanced around the room. One of the men who'd been sleeping was awake and eyed the four of us with interest. "You three need to just sit back in your chairs. Don't make it seem like we're having a conversation."

"Oh, right," Colin said excitedly. "I bet there are other secret societies who want to kill you, right?"

"Uh, no. But when your mom comes back, if she sees a forty-year-old janitor chatting with her kids, she's bound to ask what we were talking about. A degree of cloak-and-dagger is probably best until we can work out a better system." He nodded to me. "Meeting face-to-face is a necessity in our society, though. You'll be meeting everyone else soon enough."

Questions flooded my head and threatened to come charging out of my mouth, but I pressed my lips together. "Excited fear" was the best description for what I was feeling, and I didn't want to ruin what Archer would think of me by acting like a little kid. Colin and Lisa seemed to have the same thought, and the three of us did as we were told, sitting back in our chairs and looking as normal as we could manage. From our reflections in the window, we resembled criminals trying not to look like criminals.

Archer laughed and went back to scraping gum from the floor. "That'll do, I guess. It is good to finally meet you three. Especially you, Dean. You've been the topic du jour for some time. Youngest member we've ever had. There are a couple apprentices your age, but full members with the gift? Nope, you're the youngest by several years."

My questions grew by the second, and I bet I had a list as long as my crutch, but now wasn't the time to ask them all.

Archer grabbed a spray bottle and rag and started cleaning the chairs around us. "We'll have more time later, but for now, you need to know the basics." Colin moved to speak, but Archer shook his head. "We'll meet again somewhere else. The park by your house, perhaps. I'll answer your questions then." He reached into his back pocket and pulled out three business cards and slyly dropped them on my lap. I handed one to Lisa and one to Colin.

"My number's on the back." The front of the card was white with a symbol of a red circle—only not quite. It wasn't a complete circle. It stopped just short of a complete circle in the upper left portion. On the flip side were the initials "A.A." followed by a phone number.

"This is so cool," Colin said.

"You guys seem to know a bit about how things work, but let me clarify a couple things before we get interrupted," Archer began. "The most important thing to remember, Dean, is that this is a gift." His words felt like a badge that he was pinning to my chest. "An amazing gift, and you need to remember that. The *Congregatio de Sacrificio* has existed for a very, very long time. Now you are part of it."

I suddenly became very conscious of how I looked,

especially with the partly demolished cast on my leg.

"Given that you saved your sister," Archer continued, "and Mr. Peanut earlier this morning, I suspect you realize how remarkable this gift is." He drew a breath and seemed to be thinking about what to say next. For someone who belonged to an ancient secret club, he seemed to be making things up as he went. I wondered why they didn't have the "welcome to the Society" speech ironed out. But then maybe my entrance into the Society was far from the norm. Receiving the gift in a back alley from a beat-up Society member probably didn't happen too often. There'd been no time to prepare.

"As for the visions," he said after a brief pause, "you'll only have them of people you've physically touched, and only if their death is preventable. So this is really important, Dean. When someone touches you, look at them. Do what you can to learn their names. It's not always easy to do. It's especially difficult in crowds or when people are moving fast, but you need to try. Understand?"

Look at them? Learn their names? I understood what he was saying, but all kinds of questions burst into my head: What if I was at a concert and I touched a thousand people? What if I went to a wedding and had to shake hands with everyone there? What if I did everything right but just didn't remember who they were by the time I had a vision of them? I didn't want him to think I was stupid, but I had to at least ask. "Sir, what if I forget who they are?"

"Forget them?"

"Yeah, what if I bump into someone in the grocery store, get their name, and then don't have a vision of them for a year?"

"Or twenty years," Lisa added. "Dean's not exactly known for his memory. But even people with the best memories don't remember random people weeks, months, or years later."

Archer smiled. "You might forget a name, but you'll never forget a face. It's part of the gift. We're not sure how, but it does change you. I bet you recognized peanut-allergy man from when you touched him, right?"

"Bumped into him," I said. "But yeah, I did remember."

"Cool," Colin said.

Lisa chewed her lip for a moment and then asked, "What if he remembers, and we do everything we can, and we still can't... I mean, we still don't..." Her voice lowered. "What if they still die?"

Archer nodded and let out a deep sigh. "It happens, Lisa. More than we want it to. I can't tell you how to deal with that except that it's good you have close friends who understand, and now you have a society with members who will help if they can."

Lisa looked at her shoes. If she had been comforted by those words, it wasn't by much.

"Okay," Colin said, "so he'll remember the face, but does that really help track down someone you only saw once in passing a million years ago?"

"That leads me to the next thing, Dean. And this is probably the most important part. And maybe something you've already started to figure out. There are clues in the visions. You have to look very carefully at the people you see." Archer grabbed a small dustpan from his cart. "You'll see people as they are when they die. Exactly as they are."

I remembered how I'd seen Mr. Cosler's car dealership badge and how that had helped track him down.

"What they're wearing will give you clues," Archer continued. "Look closely. Are they in pajamas or tuxedos? Are there name tags, bracelets, or tattoos? Do they—"

"Dean?" My mom's voice came from behind us, and Lisa, Colin, and I leaped to our feet like we'd been caught doing something awful. Archer, though, went about his pretend business, completely unfazed. He leaned into his rag and scrubbed a section of the floor. My mom's gaze didn't even flick to him. I really needed to learn how to be that cool.

"Um, yeah, Mom?"

She raised an eyebrow, not missing our guilty faces. "You three better not be getting into trouble over there." She nodded quickly. "C'mon, they're ready for you."

CHAPTER 8

The doctor laughed when he saw my cast. Then he called in the ortho-tech, and the two of them laughed together. A couple of nurses poked their heads around the door, and before I knew it, the room was filled with people who thought that getting tackled by museum security after fighting a monk was hilarious. Perhaps if the situation had been different—like if it had happened to someone else—I'd be laughing too. But somehow, meeting Archer and having everything finally confirmed made me less ready to laugh.

I shivered for the zillionth time that day as images of past visions assaulted my mind. I'd just discovered that every person I touched was a potential nightmare. I tried to think of how many people I'd touched since the mugging that started the whole thing. Too many. Way too many. Then it hit me. The answer was so simple I wasn't sure why it had taken me so long to think of it. If touching someone connected me to them, then I just needed to make sure I didn't touch anyone.

"Ha!" The laugh burst from my lips before I realized it was coming, and the ortho-tech quickly turned off the circular saw he was using to cut the plaster off my leg. The tech gave me a concerned look, which drew a similarly worried glance from my mom. "Just tickles a bit," I said, gesturing to the saw. As he finished up, I smiled to myself. I had a plan, and by the time the last scrap of cast was off, I'd solidified my resolve: just don't touch people.

It felt strange to walk again. My leg was weak and the air seemed extra chilly against my skin. It made dodging people in the hospital corridors a bit of a challenge. Not that there were a lot of people, just that my leg seemed to move half a second slower than usual, so quick movements didn't go so well.

I managed to put some distance between me and my mom, and when I met up with Colin and Lisa I quickly told them about my no-contact plan. Lisa looked like she wanted to say something, but I cut her off with a shake of my head as my mom caught up.

Becky complained the whole way home that I'd ruined her trip to the museum. If you're an older brother to a girl, you probably realize what an amazing accomplishment that is. Score one for me. Plus, since Becky wouldn't shut up, my mom didn't pepper me with questions—another win-win. Still, she tossed an occasional glance at the rearview mirror, and I could tell she was worried. My avoidance issues would certainly be a topic she'd bring up later, probably sometime after we dropped off Colin and Lisa. I chewed my lip and decided that as long as Becky didn't bring it up, and I kept the conversation during dinner on something else, something not monk or crazy-kid related, I might have a chance at avoiding the discussion altogether.

Becky shoved another spoonful of rice into her mouth and kept on talking. "And then, after he beat up the poor monk and got his cast all busted up by the security guards, I had to sit in the parking lot for an hour while he got the rest of his cast removed."

To my dad's credit, he didn't even pause between bites as Becky recounted the events of the day, not until the very end anyway. At that point, he glanced up and gave my mom his one-raised-brow look that meant, "Is any part of that true?" My mom puckered her lips and gave an almost indistinguishable nod. Translation: "Yep, your son is a certifiable nut-job."

"That sounds like quite the day." He turned to me. "I'm sure your sister exaggerated things a bit, but is there anything you'd care to add?"

I shrugged. "It sounds bad, but it was just a stupid misunderstanding. I didn't beat anyone up. It was an accident." I gestured with my spoon across the table at my sister. "The part that you should really focus on is that your daughter is upset that she didn't get enough time with a giant piece of poop." I nodded. "That should be a bigger red flag than anything that happened to me today."

"It's not funny, Dean," Mom said.

"I'm not trying to be." I rolled my eyes. "Mom, I promise you, it was an accident. I blame the doctors for making me keep that stupid cast on my leg for longer than I needed it."

"Accident or not," my mom began, "you'll be going back there tomorrow."

I nearly choked on my spoon. "What?"

"You need to apologize to that young man."

"Who? The monk?"

"Of course the monk. That little scuffle of yours made it so he can't see the Buddha anymore." I moved to protest, but she held up a warning finger. "You should have been more respectful. After you apologize, I think you can talk to Mr. Overton, apologize to him too, and see if he'll let you and that young man into the museum again."

"But it was just an accident."

"People do apologize for accidents, Dean," my dad said. "I think it's a great idea." My mom gave an approving smile and winked at my dad.

"Ha!" Becky looked like she'd just won a contest. "Can I go too? I really want to watch Dean get beat up by a monk."

"I don't want to go back into the museum again," I mumbled.

My mom ignored my mutterings. "Plus, I think the last few weeks being cooped up indoors, away from people, has made you a little, well, socially rusty." Becky laughed again, and my mom added, "I think it would be good to reconnect with all your friends before school starts up again."

"He'd have to make some first," Becky said under her breath.

My mom gestured to my plate. "Finish your dinner. And Dean?" She tilted her head and eyed me tiredly. "No more acting out, okay?"

Acting out? As if I was the type to act out. Heck, I wouldn't act out if I was actually acting in a play and my character was told to "act out." I thought about arguing, but what would be the point? I couldn't tell them the truth, and any half-truth was just going to make my parents think I was even more nuts.

I shoved another couple of bites of food into my mouth, drained my glass of water, and smiled the most insincere, mocking smile I could manage. "I'm pretty tired. It's been a long day, and I guess I have a longer day coming my way tomorrow. I think I'll take a shower and go to bed."

I stood in the shower for a long time, thinking about the Society, thinking about Archer Astley, thinking about all the questions I had for him. How many people were in the Society? Where had it originated? How did it start? Why me? I could call Archer and set up a meeting. Or maybe he'd be waiting somewhere to talk with me. I didn't want to seem desperate, or like I was a needy little kid who couldn't cope. I didn't want them to kick me out, if that was even possible.

I walked past my parents' room after my shower and overheard my dad discussing yet another acronymic condition that I might have.

"It's possible his trauma is manifesting itself in some kind of OCD."

"Obsessive-compulsive disorder?" my mom asked.

"A mild, very treatable type," Dad said. "It'll probably resolve on its own. Dean's going to be fine. Remember that he's still just a kid too. Some of what he's going though has nothing to do with..."

I drew a breath and stopped listening, continuing to my room. Great! OCD, PTSD, ADHD, just a couple more and I'd have the whole alphabet.

Despite it all, when I hit the lights and climbed into bed, I couldn't stop myself from smiling. Sure my mom and dad thought I was nuts, and maybe my psychologist thought so too. But for the first time since the mugging that started it all, things were starting to make sense. Archer had finally made contact, and he'd explain it. I'd be part of something. Something ancient. Something important. I was still scared, but not like before. I didn't have to figure this out on my own, and that fact alone gave me hope.

Nothing could dampen my spirits.

Well, almost nothing.

CHAPTER 9

I woke up in the pitch-dark, feeling like someone was watching me. "Becky, if you're in my room, so help me..." I lunged to my right and slapped the switch on the bedside lamp. My room had faded blue walls, but as my eyes adjusted to the new light, I realized the blue had gone gray. Colin had given me a movie poster of *Attack of the 50 Ft. Woman*. It was mostly yellow, with a fifty-foot woman scooping up cars from a freeway. When I noticed the gray walls, my eyes shot to the poster; it was gray too.

Something moved to my right. My heart surged, and I turned slowly. A man in a security uniform shuffled forward and I realized it was the guard we'd met at the T. rex exhibit.

He moved another step, half a step really, and dropped his shoulder. His head jerked one way, then another, and his spine cracked as his torso bent unnaturally to the right. It was happening again, and even though not a day went by that I didn't think about my visions, I never seemed to feel fully prepared for them. I knew a scream was coming and I clenched my teeth to keep my own voice in check. Then it happened, and as the guard shrieked, my bones rattled and a muffled groan slipped past my lips.

Then, in a blink, he was gone. My gaze stayed locked where he had been, and I drew a series of deep breaths to try to calm my heart. I counted to ten, and when the color in the walls didn't return, my stomach lurched for the second time. Another person, concealed until now in the shadows, lunged forward. He was dressed entirely in black and even had one of those ski masks where you can see only eyes. I didn't have any time to gather my thoughts. The person struck the side of my bed, lunged again, and screamed at least twice as loud as the security guard. The whole time his head pivoted on its axis much farther than a human head is supposed to pivot. It was like a scene out of one of the horror movies Colin was always forcing me to watch.

I knew it wasn't real—part of me did anyway—but I didn't have time to prepare. Two visions in a matter of seconds were more than my already rattled senses could handle. And when his scream started, so did mine. His hooded face was so close that I thought I could feel his breath, which I knew was impossible given that he was a vision, but I was sure I felt it.

His shriek seemed to last longer than the others and I gathered some strength and threw myself away from the apparition and onto the floor. He was gone as suddenly as the security guard had been, and I pulled myself to my feet and leaned against my dresser. I managed two breaths before the door to my room burst open.

It was my mom. Well, I know that now, but she had on this green face mask, and her hair had pieces of cloth sticking out all over the place. She looked horrifying, so of course, I thought I was having another vision, and I screamed again. And then, to make matters even worse, she screamed, so then I was sure she was a vision. If I hadn't staggered to the side and tripped over my laundry hamper, I probably wouldn't have stopped screaming, either.

But I did—thank God—and that's when I realized the walls in my room were light blue again. I looked up from my position on the floor and saw three faces peering in from the doorway. My mom was still clutching her housecoat, my dad looked more puzzled than ever, and Becky was shaking her head.

"I'm fine!" I jumped to my feet and tried to push the image of the security guard and the guy dressed in black from my head. "I just had a nightmare, and then Mom opened the door and I thought she was some kind of swamp creature."

She drew back with a grimace and looked at my dad, who shrugged and said, "You do look rather horrifying, dear."

"It's a night mask," she said. "You were screaming

64

and—"

"Look," I said, "just don't read into this, okay? I know what you're thinking."

"That you need a straightjacket?" Becky suggested. "And maybe a tranquilizer?"

"It was just a stupid dream about… er…" I suddenly didn't know what to say. My dad was looking at me with his psychologist eyes, so any nightmare I mentioned needed to be not too scary or he'd probably be able to twist it into some deeper meaning. "Mr. Utlet," I finally said. When my mom and dad nodded, I relaxed. Nightmares about a neighbor who'd been shot a million times by the police right in front of me were expected. They'd probably have thought I was nuts if I didn't have nightmares about it.

"Are you sure you're okay, son?" my dad asked.

"I'm fine. Really."

My mom took a few steps toward me, and I stepped back involuntarily. She stopped mid-step and said, "It's just a face mask!"

"Okay," I said, still keeping my distance.

"You're sure you're okay?" she asked.

"I'm fine, Mom. Don't worry about me."

She closed the distance between us, gave me a hug, and then said something I wish she hadn't: "If you get scared again, you can sleep in our room."

"Ewww, gross." Becky cringed. "Oh my gosh, that would be the most disturbing thing ever. The whole family would need therapy. I know I would."

For the first time ever, Becky was right. "I'm fourteen, Mom. That means I'm like thirteen and a half years too old to be sleeping in your room. Please, I'm fine. I just want to go back to bed."

Becky shivered. "Dad, do you know where the camera is? I'm going to need a picture to show the therapist if he ends up sneaking into your room." She turned to me. "Maybe I'll put it on the Internet too."

My dad smiled. "He is a bit old, dear."

"Nonsense," my mom said.

Dad sighed. "Let's talk about this in the morning, shall we?"

"No, let's not," I said. "Let's never mention it, or anything about it, again. It was a bad dream. That's all. Kids have bad dreams all the time."

"At least mention it in your next therapy session, son."

I groaned. "Can't we just let it go?"

Dad shook his head. "It's important to talk about those things that seem out of character, Dean. You look like you might be a bit confused by all this, and talking can help."

Me, confused? Not anymore, but there was no point

mentioning that. For the briefest of seconds I considered telling my parents about the visions. I could tell them that the security guard was going to die. If I didn't act, then his death would be proof I was right. I know it sounds like an awful thing to think. It was only for a second.

Becky leaned around the door some more. "You do look confused. Do you even know where you are?"

"You're hilarious."

"All right, all right," my dad said. "I think it's time we all just went back to bed. Nightmares are a normal part of growing up, and Dean's witnessed some pretty traumatic things these last few months. He's got every right to have a few bad dreams."

"Thank you," I said.

He led my mom back into the hall. Becky lingered near my room, and when the door to my parents' room closed, she looked at me and shook her head. She sighed and for a moment looked genuinely concerned. "Maybe you actually do need help."

I couldn't tell if she was teasing me or being serious, and honestly, I wasn't sure which one I thought would be worse. I marched across the room and slammed my door. "Shut up, Becky."

I glanced at my bedside clock. 12:45. I figured my parents had been in my room for about five minutes, so sometime around 12:40 a.m. the security guard at the museum and some guy dressed in black were going to die. I wasn't stupid. I knew exactly what it meant.

There was going to be a burglary at the museum. One that would go very, very wrong.

CHAPTER 10

I couldn't sleep. I just lay there, shaking and wondering if I should call Archer. Every few minutes, I'd pace across the room to the window and glance out, hoping to see his ice cream truck. Then, when it was obviously not there, I'd pace back to my bed and plop down. This continued for hours, until finally, after collapsing for the umpteenth time, I closed my eyes and fell asleep. Not that it lasted.

"Dean."

"Deeeeaaaan."

Something poked me in the cheek. "Dean!"

I snapped awake with a start as the memories of the previous night flooded back. "Wha... who...?" I blinked a couple times, then rubbed my eyes. Lisa and Colin were standing at the foot of my bed. Colin was rubbing his hands and licking his lips, and Lisa was chewing her thumbnail. They knew.

"Who told you?"

"So it is true," Colin said. He pointed at Lisa. "I told you it was."

"I didn't say it wasn't true," Lisa said. "I just said your

69

sister isn't exactly a reliable source."

"Your sister?" I asked. "Jasmine?"

"Becky told her," Colin said.

"Of course she did," I groaned. Jasmine was Colin's sister and one of Becky's best friends. "Remind me to drop my sister's toothbrush in the toilet."

"Eww." Lisa grimaced. "You wouldn't really do that, would you?"

Colin waved his hands. "C'mon, man. If you've had another vision, let's hear it." He rubbed his hands together. "I've been dying for another mission."

"They're not missions," Lisa muttered. "And we just finished one, how can you already want another one?" She lowered herself to the edge of my bed. "But we better hear it anyway. Who is it? Anyone we know?"

I drew a couple deep breaths. "Okay, so it's like this..."

When I finished telling them what happened, they spoke in the same breath. "A burglary?"

"That's what I figure."

"We get to thwart a burglary!" Colin said excitedly. "This just gets better and better." He rubbed his hands. "I've always wanted to thwart something."

"I'm surprised you even know the word *thwart*," Lisa said.

"Call him," Colin said. I didn't need to ask who he meant.

I nodded and pulled out my phone and then dialed the numbers from the card. The phone rang four times before voice mail on the other end picked up:

"This is Archer." *Beep.*

The message was so abrupt that it caught me off guard. "Oh, um," I stammered, "Archer. This is Dean. Dean Curse. We met yesterday... well, you probably remember. Of course you do... um, yeah. Anyway, we were just wondering if we could meet you at the park today." I suddenly remembered the forced apology I had to give at the museum. "Erm, this afternoon if possible," I added. "Maybe around one o'clock. Okay, hope to see—" The machine beeped, cutting me off. I turned to my friends. "How was that?"

"Awkward," Colin said. "Really awkward."

"It wasn't that bad," Lisa said, "but why are we meeting him this afternoon? Group therapy is over way before that."

I groaned. "I forgot about therapy." I stretched my arms and pulled some clothes from my dresser. "My mom's making me apologize to that monk."

"The one from the museum?" Colin asked.

"No, Colin," I said, "the one from the grocery store. How many monks do you know?"

Lisa shook her head while Colin laughed. "Oh, yeah. Well, hurry up and get ready. We should get that over with as soon as possible. Are you going to say something to that security guard while we're there?"

"Just get dressed," Lisa said, pulling Colin out of my room. "We'll talk about it on the way."

I pulled on a t-shirt and jeans, ducked into the washroom to get cleaned up, and headed to the kitchen. I wasn't even five minutes behind my friends, but five minutes was plenty of time for my sister to try to make me look bad. I rounded the corner just in time to hear Becky say, "And then he screamed and asked my parents if he could sleep with them."

"What?" Lisa's eyes were the size of dinner plates.

"He did what?" Colin choked out.

Becky smiled wide. She turned to me and brought her hands up to her chin, imitating a scared, frizzy-haired brat. "Widdle Deannie got scared and wanted to sweep with his widdle mommy."

"You're such a brat," I muttered.

Lisa was still staring at me. "You wanted to sleep in your parents' bed? Really?"

"No," I sighed. "That's not what happened at all." Lisa looked unconvinced so I added, emphatically, "I didn't."

My mom strolled into the kitchen behind me and came to an abrupt stop when she saw Lisa and Colin gawking at me, and Becky sneering like the devil brat she was. "Do I even want to know?" she said. Before anyone could mutter a word, she shook her head. "Nope. I don't." She turned to me. "You almost ready? I'll drop you three off at your group meeting a little early, and you can swing by the museum on your way home."

My dad came in from outside a second later. He had a newspaper in one hand and a cup of coffee in the other. He folded the paper in half, took a careful sip of his coffee and said, "So you say you *didn't* try to hurt that monk yesterday?"

I sighed. "C'mon, Dad. I already told you I didn't. Ask anyone."

My dad nodded. "Anyone?" He seemed almost amused as he dropped the paper to the table so we could all see the front page. The headline made me groan: "Local Hero Attacks Monk." Underneath was a picture of me connecting a wicked elbow to the side of the young monk's head.

After a week of protests over the Abbotsford Museum's new Buddhist exhibit, tensions reached a boiling point when local hero Dean Curse got into a fistfight with one of the protestors: a Cambodian monk. Witnesses say it was unclear who started the scuffle, but there was no question who finished it.

"I think the monk tackled Dean to the ground," one bystander reported. "But that boy wasn't going down without a fight."

This reporter managed to speak to one of Dean Curse's schoolmates, Eric Feldman, who said, "Dean's unstable. He killed an animal with a fork once and bragged about it. I'm not surprised at all that he beat up a monk."

The curator of the museum, Mr. Jonathan Overton, said that the boys got into a little scuffle that was settled by their respective families. No property was damaged, and no one was injured.

Lisa looked at me pitifully. "Why the heck did they interview Eric?"

"I'm sure he volunteered," I said, groaning.

"At least it's a great shot," Colin said. "And to be fair to Eric, you do look like a crazy person."

"Great," I said. "Just great."

Becky shouldered her way past me holding a pair of scissors, and in a flash, she chopped the article out and held it up with a smirk. "I think I might keep a collection of crazy things Dean does," she said. "That way when the judge asks why we think he needs to be locked up, we'll have lots of proof."

"Can we please just go?" I asked.

CHAPTER 11

Group therapy was held in a dance studio, which, I have to admit, always worried me a bit. Our psychologist, Dr. Mickelsen, was a bit of a weirdo and I constantly wondered if he'd try to get us to dance about our feelings. Colin used to joke that a dance about an exploded teacher would be hilarious, but Lisa didn't really like those jokes so he only said stuff like that when we were alone. Most of the other therapy kids were already in the studio when we arrived, milling around, chatting near the circle of chairs.

"Hi, Dean." I turned and found myself facing Rylee Davis. She was a year older, in the tenth grade. She had dark hair with blonde streaks, and really big green eyes.

"Oh, hi, Rylee." I swallowed. "How's it going?"

She smiled. "Good."

Colin stepped closer to me. "Hi, Rylee."

She nodded to Colin and gave Lisa a little wave. Then she pointed at my leg. "You got your cast off."

"Oh, um, yeah. Doctors said it was all healed up, so..."

Rylee leaned close. Close enough that I could smell her watermelon lip gloss. "I saw the paper," she whispered.

I winced.

"Don't worry," she said, "I know they exaggerate. It's good to see your leg's okay, though." She smiled again and then turned and joined up with a couple other girls from the group.

"I can't believe Rylee Davis just came over and talked to you," Colin said. "She approached *you*. And that's sweet for two reasons."

I laughed nervously. "Oh, yeah?"

"For one," he said, speaking just above a whisper, "Rylee's mega hot, so you'd be the luckiest guy in ninth grade. And for two... him." He nodded across the circle and I followed his gaze to Eric Feldman, the biggest jerk in our grade. Eric glared daggers at us from across the circle and Colin gave him a mocking little wave.

"What does Eric have to do with it?" I asked.

"Are you kidding?" Colin said. "He's obsessed with her. I bet he has a giant *I LOVE RYLEE* tattoo on his back." He smiled. "Making him jealous is icing on the cake."

I hated Eric, and making him mad would be excellent—Rodney Palmer, Eric's best friend, on the other hand... I wasn't interested in making that psychopath angry. I shook my head. If Rylee liked me, it was as a friend. Besides, it's not like I could do the whole boyfriend thing *and* still manage to deal with my visions.

It *was* fun to think about, though.

I didn't realize I was smiling until Lisa stepped past me and whispered, "You're pathetic." I dropped into the seat beside her and she added, "But I think she might like you too."

"Yeah, right," I said.

"Let's get started, shall we?" Dr. Mickelsen said. He had on a blue dress shirt and a tweed coat, which was odd since it was so hot and everyone else in the room was wearing shorts and t-shirts. He started the session the same way he always did: by going around the room asking everyone to share their feelings. You could say "pass" if you didn't want to share, which was something Colin, Lisa and I used pretty much every session. But this time, when he got to me, and I said, "Pass," he didn't move on.

"Are you sure?" he asked.

I felt my eyebrows rise. "Um, yes. Very sure. Thank you."

"Nothing you're interested in talking about?"

I took another look at the therapist and realized he had a newspaper under his clipboard. My face suddenly felt warm. I swallowed and repeated, "Pass, sir."

"First he kills an animal with a fork," Eric said from across the circle, "and now he's attacking peaceful monks at libraries."

"It was at a museum, you dolt," Colin said.

"Oh, well that makes it all better, then," Eric added. He looked around the group and stopped when his gaze landed on Rylee. "It's okay to beat up monks, just so long as it's at museums."

The rest of the students in the group shifted in their seats in anticipation of what was to come. There was a tiny part of me that wanted to punch Eric. I'd done it before—right in the middle of group therapy too—and I'd be lying if I said it hadn't felt awesome. But another, larger part of me didn't care one bit what the little dweeb had to say. There was going to be a museum robbery and at least two people could die. I was pretty sure Archer would help us deal with it, but it put things in perspective a bit. I had way bigger issues than Eric Feldman and Rodney Palmer.

Colin glanced at me, and gave me a look that asked, "Are you going to punch him again?" I shook my head and leaned back and then stared Dr. Mickelsen right in the face and said, for the third time, "Pass."

Eric snorted and shook his head at me. If he did like Rylee, and he thought she liked me, he might redouble his efforts to make my life miserable. I'd have to watch out for that.

Dr. Mickelsen nodded and moved on to Colin, who said, "Pass," as did pretty much everyone else. Then he launched into a discussion about the stages of grief, and then death in general. I actually thought it was a creepier discussion than the usual creepy discussion about our exploded teacher.

"What about you, Dean?" Dr. Mickelsen asked.

I blinked. I'd missed the question. "Sorry," I said, "what was the question?"

"Well, I know we've discussed this before, but I'd like you to tell the group what you were thinking in the moments before your *accident*."

I sighed. It had been seven weeks since my "accident" and Dr. Mickelsen still said the word the way my dad did, like it was a substitute word for suicide—which it wasn't. Sure, it might have seemed like a suicide attempt, since I basically jumped into oncoming traffic, but if I hadn't done it, my sister would have been killed.

Part of me really wanted to tell the truth, say that I'd jumped in front of that car on purpose, that I was part of the *Congregatio de Sacrificio*. But talking about secret societies and admitting you had visions of people who only had twenty-four hours to live seemed terribly counterproductive when people already thought I was nuts. No, doing that would lead to more therapy, not less. I'd end up locked in a room with padded walls before I could say "antipsychotic medication."

So of course, I didn't tell them any of that stuff.

I said what everyone in the room had heard me say a dozen and a half times: "I really wasn't thinking of anything. I was just jogging across the street, and I didn't see the car. Stupid mistake. I should have looked both ways."

Eric snorted from across the circle. "He got the *stupid* part right." He elbowed Rodney, and the two of them laughed.

"Okay, boys," Dr. Mickelsen said. "That's quite enough. We don't want any more fights during therapy sessions." He looked around the group. "We have time for one more," the doctor said. "Who'd like to share?" He turned and pointed a couple chairs to my left. "Liam? Care to add something to the group?"

Liam Carter was in my grade and had been with Lisa in Mrs. Farnsworthy's history class when the explosion in the chemistry lab had obliterated the wall between the two rooms. They'd both seen Mrs. Farnsworthy die. He'd always been a sort of nervous kid, but not a complete loner. He reminded me a little of myself: not anxious to take center stage, preferring instead to blend into the background. But since the explosion, or at least since he started therapy, Liam had become almost entirely mute. He always sat in the same chair, kept his head down, and rubbed his bare arms as though he was trying to stay warm. As I looked at him, I realized how similar he and Lisa acted and I wondered if Lisa wasn't having a harder time with everything than she let on.

"What a freak," Eric said.

Liam shook his head, and Dr. Mickelsen made a note before looking out at the rest of us. "Anyone?" he asked.

I glanced at my watch and whispered, "Ten fifty-five."

"You've all made such progress," Dr. Mickelsen said, smiling. "Next week will be our last mandatory session. But I will be here every Friday, at the same time, for the rest of the summer should anyone, or everyone, decide they would benefit from some more talks." He opened his clipboard and scanned a page. "Most of you shared your thoughts today, but I hope those who didn't will share in the next session." His eyes lingered on me and he drew a deep breath and smiled. "We'll see you all next week."

"One more session," Colin said as the group dispersed. "Finally, just one more of these things. I can't wait."

As soon as I was on my feet, Eric came out of nowhere and shoved me. Hard. My leg was feeling nearly a hundred percent, but the suddenness of the shove caught me off guard and I clipped my chair with my foot and stumbled to the floor.

"That's only part of the payback," he spat.

Colin leaned forward like he was about to pound Eric, but Rodney loomed behind Eric like a thundercloud. Rodney was fourteen, but he looked eighteen. I'd known Rodney since I was nine, and I barely believed he was fourteen. He was like a science experiment gone horribly wrong. I'd say he was ogre-like, only "ogre" isn't a scary enough description for him. If ogres really existed, Rodney would be the thing that killed them. He'd kill them and then eat them and then use their bones to kill more of them. Eric would be the thing that sat on his shoulder while he did it.

Colin shrank back under the shadow of Rodney, but his hands remained in tight fists.

"What's wrong with you, Eric?" Lisa said, narrowing her eyes. "You know he only just got his cast off." The muscles in her jaw tightened, and then she sprang forward and shoved the little twerp square in the chest. He staggered back and tripped over Rodney's size twelve shoes, crumpling to the floor with a whimper.

His face reddened, and he looked, slack-jawed, first at Lisa, then up at his friend. "Are you just going to stand there?"

Rodney's gaze moved between Eric and Lisa. He reminded me of an ox, the way his head lolled one way then the next, confused and dumb. "But she's a girl," he said in a half whisper. Lisa jutted out her chin and planted her fists on her hips, glowering down at the heap of Eric on the floor.

I craned my neck to see if Dr. Mickelsen was on his way over, but the studio was pretty big and he was at the other end, standing in the entrance with his back to us, talking to some parents picking up their kids. Plus, the few remaining kids were crowding around, blocking a clear view from the door.

"C'mon," Eric said, looking up at Rodney, "do something!" His voice was half whining and half ordering.

Rodney growled and then lunged. Except he didn't lunge at Lisa. Colin stood beside her and took the full force of the shove. He hit the floor, skipping across the wood like a stone on a lake.

"What's going on over there?" Dr. Mickelsen called, finally roused from his conversation. He moved toward us cautiously, no doubt worried that Rodney would shuttle him across the floor next.

Lisa pulled me to my feet as Eric jumped to his. He pointed at the two of us. "This isn't over," he growled. "We're not even. Not even close." He stormed off with Rodney trailing him just as Dr. Mickelsen arrived.

"Well?" the doctor said. He watched Eric and Rodney leave the studio before turning back to us. "What was that about?"

I shook my head. "Nothing." Eric and Rodney may have been royal pains, but telling on them would only accomplish two things, neither of them good: Eric and Rodney would want even more revenge, and Dr. Mickelsen would inform his good friend and fellow psychologist, my dad. I needed the spotlight off me. Getting into fights wasn't the way to do that.

"What about you?" the doctor asked, looking at Colin. "Care to explain what you were doing on the floor?"

"Tripped," Colin answered, brushing off. "I'm just clumsy like that."

Lisa hauled me to my feet and then grabbed Colin's arm. "Thanks for the session," she said, talking to Dr. Mickelsen as she pulled us toward the door. "See you next week."

CHAPTER 12

We caught a bus a block away from the dance studio and headed back to the museum. I was dreading the apology, and it seemed the universe was in sync with my mood: heavy gray clouds rolled across the sky, blocking out any trace of the sunny summer day we'd started out with. I just wanted to get it over with.

When we rounded the corner and caught sight of the museum, I nearly fainted. The small mob of protestors from the day before had grown. A lot.

Lisa gasped. "There must be fifty people over there."

I would've guessed a hundred. The whole area was packed like a rock concert. The crowd didn't fit at a museum. The protestors were on the curb, separated from the entrance by the museum's manicured lawn. Police paced between the protestors and the museum, and news vans with satellite dishes protruding from their roofs filled the parking lot.

"I bet more than a hundred," Colin said, a grin slowly spreading across his face. He grabbed my shoulder excitedly. "I bet it's because of that article."

I groaned. Rumors of the insane kid who attacked a

monk had probably started spreading as soon as I had been hauled off by security the previous day. Now the article made it all true. Every single protestor probably thought I was some kind of racist monk-hater.

"I can't go in there, guys. They'll kill me."

Lisa stood back and tapped her chin. She snatched the Red Wings ball cap off Colin's head and slapped it on mine.

"Hey!" Colin said. "What gives?" He rubbed his hands over his head, trying, with zero success, to smooth out all the chunks of hair sticking up from his head.

Lisa smirked.

"What?" Colin asked. "I didn't think I'd have to brush my hair since I was planning on wearing my hat."

"Dean needs it more than you," Lisa said.

"A hat?" I shook my head. "A hat isn't going to be a good enough disguise. I'll be spotted as soon as I cross the street."

"No, you won't," Lisa said. "The photo with the article wasn't very clear, and even if it was, they'll be looking for a kid with a cast and a pair of crutches." She gestured to Colin's head. "Plus they'll be too busy staring at Colin's hair to even notice you." She turned to Colin and smirked. "You look like a hobo."

For some reason, everything except the hobo part sounded perfectly reasonable. They would be looking for a kid in a cast, certainly a kid with crutches. In fact, the more I thought about it, the more I was convinced they wouldn't expect to see me. What kind of crazy kid would come back to the scene of the crime only twenty-four hours after the fact? I'd wear the hat just to be safe, but yeah, I bet I wouldn't even be noticed with all the excitement going on over there.

Colin seemed to register my acceptance and sighed. "Fine. You can use the hat. But you owe me."

"Thanks," I said.

"Okay." Lisa chewed her lip and turned back to the museum. "What do we do first? See the curator or go talk to the monk?"

"Mr. Overton," I said. "If things go bad talking to the monk, we may have to run, and I don't want to have to sneak back." I paused and then added, "You don't think the monk thinks I hit him on purpose, do you? Because if he does, he'd probably want to—"

"Whack you with something?" Colin finished.

I nodded. "Yeah, like his fist."

We went around the block and crossed through the parking lots of neighboring businesses to avoid having to shove our way through the protestors. But when we rounded the corner of the building, we ran straight into more people, this time standing in line.

I gasped. "More protestors?"

An older man with a scruffy face and a plaid flat cap, standing at the back of group, turned. I instinctively lowered my head so he couldn't see my face, and Colin and Lisa stepped up like a couple of Secret Service operatives and stood shoulder-to-shoulder in front of me.

"Protestors?" he asked. "No, those are the protestors." He pointed toward the mob on the street. "We're just waiting in line." He raised his voice and directed it at the angry mob. "We're not like those nutters!"

Several of the protestors shouted, shaking their fists and raising signs.

"Let's not antagonize them, sir," an authoritative voice said from the right. I tilted my head. It was one of the security guards from the previous day, not the one from my vision, but one who would probably recognize me. Who was I kidding? They probably had a picture of me at the ticket counter with a note to TASER ON SIGHT if I was stupid enough to return. My mom had called ahead, I reminded myself. It should be okay.

"Yeah, yeah," the old guy said. "Don't antagonize them. Heaven forbid we antagonize those loons."

A few older teenagers pushed their way through the protestors and joined the line behind us. "Awesome," a girl with light blue hair and an eyebrow ring said.

"I know, right?" another girl in the group said.

I recognized the second girl's voice and practically

choked. It was Rylee. I turned my body and lowered the brim of my cap.

"I can't wait to see this head thing," the blue-haired girl added.

I felt a tinge of guilt. That monk hadn't liked the way we had gawked at the relic, and now, thanks to that stupid article, it was getting more attention than ever. It wasn't really my fault. Was it?

I risked a quick glance up to see if the guard had left and ended up locking eyes with him. I jerked my head away and turned my attention to the brick wall on my right, picking at it as though it was the most interesting thing I'd ever seen.

"Dean?" It was Rylee's voice from behind me. "Dean, is that you?"

I hunched over and looked down at the concrete and shook my head.

Lisa laughed nervously. "Hi, Rylee. No, no, this isn't Dean."

"Yeah," Colin said. He dropped his voice to just above a whisper. "Dean wouldn't want to be spotted here after the incident in the paper." There was a pause and I imagined him giving Rylee a wide-eyed *please play along* look. Then he said, "So, uh, what brings you guys here?"

Nice, I thought, change the subject.

"Who is that, then?" another girl pressed. The

officer's thick-soled boots stepped closer, and even though I didn't look up, I felt his gaze boring into me.

"Who?" Colin asked, his voice cracking. There was an awkward silence, and I suddenly felt Colin grab my shoulder. "Oh, this is... erm..."

"It's just..." Lisa began.

"Just... my little sister," Colin said.

Lisa groaned, and Rylee and her friends snickered. I imagined everyone around us was looking at me. I wanted to spin around and kick Colin right in the shins, but instead I just clenched my fists and tried to make myself smaller and more sister-like. Colin was a great friend, and he always had my back, but sometimes he just said the stupidest things.

"You two look familiar." This time it was the guard. Colin sounded like he was about to say something, but the guard added, "Yeah, you were here yesterday. You're friends with that crippled kid who beat up that monk."

"He didn't actually beat up the—" Lisa abruptly stopped as the guard took another step forward. The whole area fell silent. I tried to press myself into the bricks. A large hand gripped the brim of my cap and turned my head slowly around and then finally lifted the hat off my head.

"Your sister sure is pretty," the girl with the blue hair mocked, while her friends snickered. Rylee gave me an apologetic look.

The guard seemed pleased. "Overton said you'd be coming by, but I thought you'd change your mind when you saw them." He nodded to the protestors.

"Starting to wish I had," I muttered. I became aware of the attention directed my way from the other people in the line and considered sprinting away and hiding under a rock somewhere.

"Is that the kid from the paper?" a woman's voice asked.

"It looks like him, but he had crutches in the paper," another voice said.

"You think he's here to fight that monk again?" a young voice asked.

"You think he'll give me his autograph?"

My cheeks burned. The security guard placed a hand on my shoulder and pulled me from the line. "Okay, kid," he said. "Let's go."

"What about my friends?" I asked, pointing back.

Lisa and Colin stepped out of the line, intending to follow us, but the guard raised his free hand. "Uh-uh. You two can stay here. Or wait in line and go visit the museum, or do anything you want. Overton said he wanted to speak to Mr. Curse, so you'll see him when the meeting is over."

"Now just wait a—" Colin started to say, but the guard cut him short.

"Don't worry, kid," the officer said with an evil smirk. "Your little sister will be out before you know it."

CHAPTER 13

The walls of Mr. Overton's office were hung with certificates, diplomas, the odd painting of some abstract scene, and several old, faded portraits of angry men and women. Previous curators, I imagined. There were several artifacts around the room; some of the smaller ones were on shelves or ledges. An odd collection of thick chains and heavy locks was piled up in one of the corners. If it hadn't looked like they had been placed there with some care, I might have thought Mr. Overton used chains and locks as a regular part of his meetings. I was about to stand up from the leather chair I was in to investigate the oddity a bit more when the office door opened and in walked Mr. Overton.

"Dean!" A smile spread across his face, and he crossed the five or six meters between the door and my chair before I had a chance to stand. "My boy, it's good to see you."

"It is, sir?"

He reached out and grabbed my hand before I could shove it in my pocket and gave it several enthusiastic pumps. *Great,* I thought, *more physical contact. Yet another person I have to worry about dying.*

"Of course it is, Dean."

"Then... you're not upset at me for what's going on outside? You don't blame me?"

Mr. Overton gave the top of my head a rub, then moved to his desk and sat on the corner. "Oh, you bet I do," he said. "You get full credit for that, young man. Full credit indeed."

"Oh." I felt like reminding him that the protestors had been out there long before my little incident, but I decided it would probably only make matters worse. So instead I said, "That's why I'm here, sir. I wanted to apologize for my actions. It was all a big misunderstanding. Just a silly accident. But clearly, it's made some challenges for you, and I guess for that monk too."

"Challenges?" Mr. Overton waved his hand. "You mean the protestors? Nonsense."

I blinked. "Nonsense?"

"Nonsense," he repeated, looking very pleased. "I owe you a debt of gratitude, young man."

"You do?"

"We've had that artifact on display for almost two weeks, and guess how much it increased attendance?"

"I... I don't have a clue, sir. Lots?"

"None." He shook his head. "Sure, it was in the papers because of the protestors, but it never made the top story, never front page. Even the local newspaper buried it on page six. Page six!" he repeated dejectedly.

"That's the Community Arts section. The write-up about the Buddha head was underneath an article about how the community theatre was doing *The Wizard of Oz* for the hundredth time. Even our coprolite exhibit drew more attention than the Buddha head, and that head cost us almost a quarter of our annual budget."

"I don't understand," I managed to say.

"I'll admit it, Dean. Yesterday I thought your little scuffle was going to make even fewer people come here. But did you see the line outside?"

I nodded.

He jumped up, paced to the window, and looked out. "It's huge. I can't remember the last time we've actually had that kind of line. And did you see the newspaper this morning?"

I groaned inwardly.

"Of course you did," he said quickly. "Front page. Finally!"

"So it's a *good* thing, what happened yesterday?"

"I know I banned you, Dean, but consider that ban lifted. You're welcome here anytime."

I sighed. "Oh, I'm so glad to hear that. I've been feeling bad for causing that monk to get kicked out. My mom said it's probably pretty important for him to see that artifact every day."

"Oh, well," the curator began, *"he's* still banned—

actually, they all are."

"But you said—"

"Dean, they were making it uncomfortable for patrons to view the artifact long before you came into the picture. There were other complaints. I need to make sure that doesn't happen again. The artifact is on loan, you know. We only get it for a month. That means we only have two weeks left. Plus, quite a few of those protestors are here because Mr. Pran was kicked out, and all the news crews are here because of your little altercation. If I let the monks back, things will just go back to normal." He shook his head. "Normal is not good." He smiled. "Do you know there are even groups of protestors walking around the whole block with their angry little signs for everyone who drives by to see? It's the cheapest advertising we've ever gotten."

"But, sir," I said, "isn't that relic important to those monks? I mean, aren't you kind of taking advantage of them?"

"It's just two more weeks, Dean. Then they'll get to see the artifact as much as they want." He checked his watch. "I'm afraid I have some meetings this morning, but I'm glad you stopped by. Don't worry about the monks. They'll follow the relic to the next museum, and I'm sure they'll get to spend all the time they want with it there." He opened the door and stood to the side.

It wasn't exactly what my mom had wanted me to

accomplish, but I had to admit I felt a lot better. It had been an accident, and while I owed the monk an apology, which I'd give him soon enough, it wasn't like he'd never be allowed to see his precious relic again—just not for two weeks. He couldn't be too upset about that. It wasn't exactly *fair*, but I'd done what I could do. I took a step through the door and suddenly remembered my vision. The security guard's twisted face filled my mind.

"Mr. Overton," I said, turning back to the curator, "I'd like to apologize to the officer from yesterday. I think his name was Fisher?"

"Fisher, Fisher..." He tapped his chin. "Oh, yes, Mr. Fisher is on the night shift today, so he won't be starting until eight. I believe he works most Sundays during the day, though. Perhaps you can stop by over the weekend."

"Yeah, right. He'll be dead by then," I muttered.

The curator's eyes widened. "Come again?"

"Oh, um." I scrambled for a lie. "I just said that I'd probably be in bed by then."

Mr. Overton blinked twice and gave his head a quick shake. "Right, well, he'll probably be here most of the day on Sunday, so when you wake up, come on down. I'm sure he'll appreciate the apology."

"Okay. Thank you, sir. I'll be sure to stop by."

He rubbed my head again as I turned back to the hallway and left the room. I hate it when people rub my head.

CHAPTER 14

"He wasn't mad?" Colin asked after I'd found him and Lisa and told them how things had gone.

"Nope," I said. "He thanked me."

Lisa's face scrunched. "What a jerk."

"What?" I asked. "A jerk? Why? He didn't get me in trouble. He said I'm welcome anytime."

"He's exploiting those monks to make the museum more popular, Dean. In fact, he's a double jerk, since that was his goal all along. The whole reason he brought that artifact here to begin with was probably to get protestors."

"I agree with Lisa," Colin said, "and I don't do that if it can be helped." Sarcastic or not, Colin's comment seemed to be appreciated by Lisa. Her lips pursed with resolve, and she nodded quickly.

I shrugged. "Okay, so he's a jerk. Nothing we can do about it. I said I was sorry. I asked if the monk could be allowed back in, and he said no. It would be bad for business, I guess."

"Bad for business?" Lisa said through clenched teeth. "Bad for business?" Her hands curled into fists at her sides. "Maybe we should just go tell those news people what he said."

I groaned. "C'mon, Lisa. Forget about it. It's just two weeks. The monks probably don't even care." She gave me a look that could have frozen hot water, but I ignored it... or at least tried hard to.

Colin piped up. "Let's just find that bald kid, apologize, and then go meet up with Archer. I think the upcoming museum heist and two deaths are a bit higher up on the list of important things."

Lisa crossed her arms over her chest and huffed. "The museum deserves to be robbed. Maybe we shouldn't even try to stop it."

"We're not trying to stop *it*, Lisa." Stress added an edge to my voice. "We're trying to stop two people from dying, remember?"

She blushed and looked at the ground.

"Now I agree with Dean," Colin said. "Let's get this apology nonsense over with so we can go talk to Archer. We need to learn more about magic societies, blood rites, and sacred oaths."

I blinked. "Magic? Blood rites? You have to stop watching all those conspiracy movies, Colin. The Society doesn't have any of those things."

"Are you sure?" He tilted his head slowly until his ear was pressed firmly to his shoulder and his eyes were as wide as he could make them, then he lowered his voice and spoke with a spooky tone. "Are you *really* sure?"

"You have problems," I said.

"I saw a couple of the monks when we were in line," Lisa said. "The young one is probably with them. Just keep your head down and Colin and I will bring you close to him so you can say you're sorry."

"Keep my head down? Like I did in the line? Yeah, that worked pretty well. No one recognized me at all."

As if on cue, an angry male voice spoke up from behind me. "Hey, you're that kid. The one from the newspaper."

I instinctively lowered my head and let Colin and Lisa step up to block me from the voice.

"Nope," Colin said, "my... little *brother* hasn't ever been in the newspaper." I guess I should have been grateful that I was at least Colin's brother rather than his sister, but I didn't know why he didn't just say I was his friend.

"Hey, guys," the man called. "Over here."

The man was waving over a group of twenty people or so. Some of them had signs held over their heads. As the group started walking toward us, I decided it was time to move on and promptly jogged away.

"Where are you going?" the man shouted. "I was talking to you." There was a pause, and I imagined that the man was telling everyone who I was. More angry shouts came from the group, but I didn't bother to acknowledge them.

Lisa nudged me toward a small grove of trees on the chunk of lawn that separated the museum from the street. It was far enough from the building that the protestors probably wouldn't be interested in it, and since it was off the sidewalk, we might not be noticed.

"Just ignore them," Lisa said once we were standing beneath the branches.

"Yeah," Colin said. "Half those people are crazy, and the other half would probably protest a new traffic light for being too controlling." He thought for a second and then added, "But I guess your disguise isn't really as good as I thought it was."

"My disguise is a hat," I said. "That doesn't qualify as a disguise in anyone's book."

"Just wait here," Colin said. "Lisa and I will go see if we can find the monk and get him to come over here." He nodded to Lisa. "Right?"

Lisa didn't answer. Her attention was fixed on something in the small park across the street. "Is that...?"

I followed her gaze to the small patch of green. Something orange moved between the branches of the trees and shrubs around the park's perimeter.

"What?" I said, squinting. I blinked and finally realized what Lisa was looking at. The orange was the distinctive color of the robes the monks wore, and sure enough, a second later, a monk paced past a small break in the trees, then turned and disappeared behind them again.

It was just enough time for us to see it was the young monk.

Colin nudged me. "C'mon, let's get this over with."

I bit my lip and nodded.

CHAPTER 15

The park wasn't really a park. It was too small for that. It was the size of a classroom. The green space was enclosed in a chain-link fence lined with chest-high bushes. Saplings, about the height of a basketball net, were evenly spaced around the perimeter, and the monk was speaking to a man in casual street clothes, positioned behind one of the slender trunks. We were too far away to hear anything, but it was clear by the way the monk was swinging his hands and pointing angrily at the museum that he wasn't happy. It probably had to do with being kicked out of the building.

"That was easy," Colin said. He looked at Lisa and then me. "C'mon, what are we waiting for?"

"He doesn't look too happy," I said. The monk had to be at least a year older than us, and he was a bit bigger than me, so I was pretty sure he'd be upset about how the newspaper had made him look. "He might still be mad. Maybe it's better if I just write him a note."

"You're not writing him a note," Lisa said, prodding me forward. "Let's hurry up before someone spots you."

As we moved toward the crosswalk, I realized that the monk was actually completely hidden from the view of anyone standing near the museum. In fact, if we hadn't been standing at the grove on the edge of the property, we'd never have spotted him. We approached slowly once we were on the other side of the street. Even Lisa, who I thought was feeling pretty confident about the whole thing, shifted from a brisk march to the tips of her toes once the muffled voices drifted over the fence. It wasn't until we were a meter or two from the actual fence that their voices became clear. They weren't speaking English, but I recognized the language from school.

"They're speaking French," Lisa whispered. "Not Khmer."

"Khmer?" Colin looked puzzled.

"That's what they speak in Cambodia."

"How do you know that?" Colin whispered.

Lisa waved her hand at him to shut up, and the three of us inched closer to the fence until our faces were almost pressed against the chain links. I wasn't really sure why we were trying to eavesdrop on the conversation, but it seemed like the most practical thing to do for some reason.

"*D'accord, nous le ferons ce soir,*" a man's voice said.

I searched my mind for a translation. I'd taken French an hour a day since kindergarten, like pretty much everyone I knew, but French wasn't my thing, and honestly, I was lucky if I could introduce myself properly. Lisa was different, though. Her parents had sent her to Quebec for a month a few years ago, and she'd come back speaking better than anyone in our class. I looked at her expectantly.

"Well?" I whispered.

She pressed her fingers to her lips and leaned a bit farther over the fence. I did the same, even though it really didn't matter how close I got. They could speak through a megaphone and it wouldn't be any easier for me to understand.

"*Qu'est-ce que c'était?*"

Lisa stood up straight as a bolt just a second before the hedge parted and I came face-to-face with the young monk.

His eyes narrowed as he stared at me, and then he let out an exasperated sigh. "Oh, of course." The man he was talking to turned abruptly, jogged the few meters across the tiny park, and vaulted the fence on the other side, leaping through the bushes without hesitation. I turned back and found the monk glaring at me. "What do you want?" he asked.

"I... I, um, I just... you speak French?"

He rolled his eyes. "No." The hole in the bushes vanished, but the monk's voice flitted through the leaves. "Now get lost."

I groaned. I was here to deliver an apology, and that's what I was going to do. Flanked by Lisa and Colin, I marched down the fence line, pushed through the gate, and continued across the grass, only faltering when the monk turned to face me. He put his fists on his hips, his orange robes draping over his body like heavy blankets, and I was reminded once again of all the kung fu movies I'd seen at Colin's house.

He glared at me for a few long seconds until I swallowed and spoke. "Look," I said with a sigh. "We got off on the wrong foot yesterday. I'm not the kind of guy who makes fun of important things, and I really am sorry about what happened."

The monk looked up at the leaves of one of the saplings and drew in a long, slow breath. He let it out in a single burst. Then he extended his hand. "I'm Sokhem," he said. "Sokhem Pram. But most of my friends back home just call me Sok."

I stared at his outstretched hand, wondering if I really wanted to make contact with someone else, but then I remembered that we'd already had plenty of contact. I smiled at his name, but didn't laugh. "I'm Dean Curse," I said, grabbing his hand and shaking it. "And these are my friends, Lisa and Colin."

Colin snickered. "Nice to meet you, *Sok.*"

The monk rolled his eyes. "It's S-O-K, not S-O-C-K." He turned to me. "I know you weren't trying to hit me yesterday. And you weren't really that rude. It's just... it gets frustrating. I can't really go home until we get the relic back, and as long as people want to see it, the museum won't even consider our requests." He gave his head a shake. "Anyway, I took out my frustration on you guys first, so I guess I'm sorry too."

"Home?" Colin asked. "To Cambodia?"

"No, London," Sok replied.

That explained the English accent. I scratched the back of my head. "You're a Cambodian monk from London? And you speak French?"

"I was born in Cambodia, but I grew up in London. I live there with my mum. I promised my grandfather..." He opened a hole in the bushes and pointed at the three robed men standing to the side of the protestors in front of the museum. "That's him on the right; he's the one who taught me French. Anyway, I promised him I'd spend a few months as a monk in the monastery in his village over summer vacation. But before I got there, the artifact was stolen and it turned up not long after in Amsterdam." He shook his head. "That was almost three months ago. I was supposed to be back in London by now. But like I said, my grandfather doesn't want me to leave until we have it back."

"Is there anything we could do to help?" Lisa asked.

Sok turned and gave a weak laugh. "No."

"That's it?" Lisa asked when Sok didn't elaborate. "Just, *no*?"

"Look," Sok began, "I appreciate the thought, but

we've tried everything. A stolen artifact from a tiny little village in Cambodia isn't top priority for anyone. Especially when our only proof is a couple blurry photographs and the eyewitness accounts of three very old monks."

"They don't believe them?" Colin asked.

Sok shook his head. "And all the protests seem to make matters worse. They just generate more interest, and the more interest the statue gets, the more the museum wants to keep it. We've raised some money, though—enough to buy it back—but they won't sell it." He waved his hand. "It doesn't matter, I've made arrange-ments—" He cut himself off abruptly, and his gaze flicked across the park to where the French-speaking man had disappeared. "To go back to London in a couple weeks," he added finally.

"You're just giving up on it?" Lisa asked. "But what about your grandfather?"

He shrugged. "I said he doesn't *want* me to leave, not that I'm a prisoner. I have school. I've done everything I can. He'll just have to get over it."

Sok didn't seem as upset as I thought he should be, but what did I know? Maybe he was just accepting the inevitable. Lisa and Colin continued to ask Sok questions, but their voices faded into the background as a new thought hit me: the robbery. I tilted my head and scrutinized Sok, trying to determine if he was capable of pulling off a grand heist. I focused on his eyes and pulled up the mental image of the masked guy in my vision. After a minute, I blinked. I had seen nothing of the man in my vision but the eyes; I hadn't even noticed how tall he was. I shook my head. The museum was stocked full of valuable items. Things like gold, jewelry, and paintings, and I'd bet all of those would be a million times more valuable than a Buddha head.

No. People were going to die, I reminded myself. A security guard and a thief, and even though Sok looked like he could get pretty angry, he didn't look like a killer.

Sok nodded when we were done talking, and strolled away through the gate and out of the park.

"That went well," Colin said.

Lisa parted the bushes around the fence and watched Sok jog across the street. "You guys don't think that he's the..."

"I thought the same thing," I said. "But I don't think so. He doesn't really strike me as the killer type."

"It's just," Lisa continued, "that man who ran away, did you guys hear what he said?"

"I heard him," Colin said, "but I didn't understand him."

"He said, '*Nous le ferons ce soir,*'" Lisa repeated with a French accent. "That means, 'Let's do it tonight.'"

"It does?" Colin asked.

"They could have been talking about anything," I said. "It might be entirely innocent." I only half believed my own words. My mind was already flipping through various scenarios in which Sok used the money the village had raised to buy back the relic to hire a thief to steal it back. Maybe his mystery friend would get into a scuffle with an armed guard and a gun would go off—accidentally or otherwise. Plus, it wasn't like Sok and his mystery friend were meeting out in the open, and that guy had run away pretty quick when we'd shown up at the playground.

I shook my head. "It doesn't matter. We need to talk to Archer, and he'll help us figure this out. It'll be fine." I told that to myself again and again and planned to keep telling myself until I believed it.

Colin tapped his watch. "Let's get to the park. I've wanted to talk to Archer all day long. I think maybe he can get us some crime-fighting tools. Like grappling hooks and throwing stars and x-ray glasses and—"

"He's not a spy," Lisa said with an exasperated sigh.

The two of them argued as we crossed the park and made our way down the street toward the bus stop. Just before we rounded the corner, I glanced back. Sok was standing at the corner of the building, peering curiously down an alley between the museum and the bakery.

Could it be him? I wondered. *Could he be the guy from my vision?*

CHAPTER 16

The idea that Sok might be the burglar hung in my head like a neon sign. I couldn't ignore it. Lisa and Colin were thinking the same thing, and argued while we rode the bus.

"He's a monk, Colin. There's no way he'd do that," Lisa said.

"We could tie him up," Colin suggested, ignoring Lisa completely. "He can't get killed if he's tied up."

Lisa rolled her eyes at having been ignored and said, "Even if he was the burglar, and I still don't think he is, you can't just tie him up. If you think you make the front page for hitting a monk, what do you think they'd do for kidnapping one? What if we just tell him that if he tries to steal from the museum he's going to die?"

Colin laughed. "Tying him up would be better, and we'd probably seem less nuts."

"We can't count on the fact that he's the burglar," I said finally, as the bus came to a stop beside the park. "It's him or it isn't, and if we waste our time stopping him from doing something that he wasn't ever going to do in the first place, well, we won't have stopped anything. Besides,

I bet Archer has stopped dozens of robberies. There's probably a policy in place for this sort of thing. A trick or something that works every time." I followed them off the bus. "Let's just find him and get a real plan."

Colin and Lisa nodded in agreement. I think they could sense my escalating stress. I had only a few hours left to intervene. What kind of stupid *gift* only gives you twenty-four hours to act, anyway? Why not forty-eight? Why not a week?

Finding Archer wasn't difficult. The gray clouds that had been rolling around the sky barely an hour before had become a menacing blanket blocking out any trace of blue, and reducing the number of kids in the park to a handful. Also, Archer was in an ice cream truck, so we just followed that annoying little jingle. We found him pulled over beside a large play area where a handful of older kids were doing stunts on the swings.

He smiled and rested his elbows on the sill of the window cut into the side of his truck. "Well, well," he said, "if it isn't the angry monk-beater."

Lisa and Colin laughed stiffly, but I could only manage a weak grin. Time was slipping away, and we didn't have a plan yet. Archer's smile slid off his face. It was clear he noticed that something wasn't right.

"What's wrong?" he asked.

"Dean had another vision," Lisa said.

"A bad one," Colin added.

"They're seldom good," Archer said, leaning out the window, "but let's hear it."

My hands shook as I stepped a bit closer. I wasn't sure if I was nervous about talking to Archer or scared about dealing with another vision.

I clenched my fists and told him everything. Archer didn't say a word while I spoke, and Lisa and Colin only interjected once to expand on my thought that maybe, just maybe, Sok was the burglar. When I was done, Archer disappeared into his truck and returned a few seconds later with three ice cream treats. Then he just stood there, lost in thought, until he finally said, "So, what do you think you should do?"

I flinched. "What do I think *I* should do? I... I mean, we were hoping that maybe *you'd* handle this."

Archer's brow rose.

"I mean, it's just that we're talking about a robbery, right? A museum robbery. Those guards have guns."

Archer stood up and puffed out his skinny chest. "I may look bulletproof, but I'm quite fragile."

"But haven't you done stuff like this before?" Colin asked.

"Stopped a museum robbery?" Archer smiled. "Nope. This would be the first." He leaned over again and stared at me, his lips set in a thin line. "You've been kind of thrust into this, Dean, and I'm sorry about that. But we need to get you ready, and believe it or not, this is one case you don't need me to take care of for you."

"What?" Lisa's eyes bugged out. "You're not going to help?" Her voice drew glances from the few kids still in the playground, and she blushed and inched back a step.

"Mr. Astley, please," I begged. "The last time we tried to intervene with robbers, things didn't go well."

Archer shook his head. "Don't blame yourselves. All things considered, you didn't do too badly." Before I could state the obvious, that my neighbor had died and so we had in fact done quite badly, Archer continued. "I know the outcome wasn't perfect, but I've seen far more experienced members fail at far easier missions. In the end, though, you need to remember it wasn't your fault."

Lisa bit her lip and cast a nervous glance at me, and then she turned back to Archer and spoke, but her words came out almost like a whimper. "You're really not going to help us?"

"I didn't say I wouldn't help you," Archer said. "I just said I wouldn't be taking care of it for you. I'm here to help you. That's my job."

The three of us sighed with relief, and Colin slapped a hand on my shoulder.

"But this one's easy," Archer continued. "You know the security guard works at the museum, and you can be pretty sure the man in black is a thief. You know the when, the where, and the what." He looked at us expectantly. "So what do you think you should do?"

"Tie up the monk," Colin said.

Archer's mouth twisted. "Yeah... maybe we should come back to that option." He gave me a worried look and added, "Since you're not even sure it was this monk—what did you say his name was again?"

"Sok," Lisa said. "Sok Pram."

Archer nodded. "Right. Well, Sok might not be the thief." His eyebrows rose. "This is simple. Forget Dean's gift. You know the when and where of a crime that's going to be committed so..."

"The police?" I asked.

"We can't go to the police," Colin said. "They'll think we're nuts."

Archer shrugged. "They might. But if you can convince them there is a sliver of truth to your story, they'll check into it. And even an increased police presence can be effective at stopping crime."

"But if we can't tell them about Dean's vision," Lisa said, "then we... what? Lie?"

Archer blew out a breath and rubbed his chin. "There are some people in the Society who don't lie on principle. I have a slightly different moral compass. A lie to save a life? I wouldn't lose sleep over that. But it's something you'll have to decide on your own."

I'd lied to my parents dozens of times since I got the gift... and to so many other people along the way too. I wondered when I'd gotten so comfortable lying, and why I didn't feel worse about it. The only thing I could come up with was that, like Archer said, a lie to save a life hardly seemed wrong. "I guess I don't have too much of a problem lying," I said finally.

"A quick piece of advice then," Archer said. "The best lies are the simplest lies. Don't make them complicated. Just short and simple. You don't want to give them something to poke holes in."

"Tips on how to lie," Lisa said. "What's next, lock-picking lessons?"

"If you like," Archer said without a hint of sarcasm.

"Cool," Colin said.

I took a deep breath. We didn't have a fully formed plan, but we had something, and the knot in my stomach relaxed some. Archer was right. If the police drove around the block a few times, or swung by a few minutes before the break-in, the burglars would either be arrested or they'd just change their minds and leave. Sok's image suddenly popped into my head. If he was the burglar, I hoped he'd see the police and leave. For some reason, I didn't want him to get caught, which was a bit strange since I hardly knew the guy.

Thunder cracked, and a single raindrop struck my cheek, pulling me back to the moment at hand. "Okay," I said. "I think we can handle it."

"I think you can too," Archer agreed. "But if something happens and you need my help, call me."

More raindrops hit my face, and I glanced up at the dark sky.

"We have other questions," Colin said.

"I thought you would," Archer said. "Ask away."

CHAPTER 17

"Is there a secret lair somewhere?" Colin asked excitedly. "Like Batman's cave, the X-Men's mansion, or Justice League's Watchtower, or—"

"He watches a lot of movies," I explained as Archer's eyes widened.

"I see," Archer said with a grin. "That's not a bad question, Colin. I've often thought that the Society needed some kind of secret hideout. Like maybe a command centre in an abandoned subway tunnel—retrofitted of course."

"That would be so cool," Colin said dreamily.

"We have a place we meet," Archer said, "but I think you'll find it's not quite up to the standards of the Bat Cave. It serves its purpose. We work together when the situation requires it, which isn't often. A chairman is appointed—the current one lives in England—and he and his team run things on a global scale, but there are country leaders, and within the countries are zones and districts. It's all very boring, I'm afraid. But it's necessary."

"Can we see it?" Colin asked, almost begging. "The meeting place, I mean."

"Of course," Archer said. "There's a meeting not too far off, actually. You three can come with me if we can think of something to tell your parents."

Colin's grin practically tore his face in half.

"So I'll only have visions of people I touch, right?" It was a point I felt needed to be fully understood. If I was going to act like a nut avoiding people, I wanted to make sure it was going to work.

"And only if he can do something about it," Lisa added, "right?"

Archer nodded. "Pretty much."

"Pretty much?" I asked. "Does that mean *yes*?"

"It's not quite so cut and dry; even among Society members debates rage about this issue. Here's how I see it: I imagine that every person I make a connection with—every person I touch—is connected to me by a guitar string. So imagine you're standing in a field with hundreds of thousands of strings connecting you to hundreds of thousands of people. The better I know that person, or the closer that person is in proximity to me, the more in tune that string is." He licked his lips. "Then I imagine that when someone I am connected to is going to suffer a deadly—preventable—fate, Death plucks that string of the guitar."

"Death?" Lisa asked. "As in hooded figure in a black robe, carries a scythe?"

"That's the one," Archer said. "In the figurative sense,

of course. Now that first note, that's the vision. It's strong, it's direct, it's as if Death himself is sending out a warning. The second warning…" He shook his head. "That one's tough. If you know the person really well, if your connection to that person is really strong—or you're in really close proximity—that second note can be just as strong. But if you're not close, if you're not *that* connected, the warning is weak, or often nonexistent." He looked at us carefully then asked, "Does that make some sense?"

I remembered the first couple of people I touched and how I had visions of them and then read about their deaths in the paper. There hadn't been any second warning with them, I hadn't experienced Death's second note in those cases. But then I wasn't anywhere nearby, and I'd never truly met the people before. "Yeah," I said. "I get it."

Archer smiled, then took a breath and continued. "Now let's say you make a connection with someone ten minutes before they're going to step out in front of a bus. You won't get that first warning. Death played that first note before you were connected. But you'll still get the second warning note."

"How will he know who to save?" Colin asked. "It could be anyone, right?"

"Yeah, Colin, it could. But remember, in those situations where you miss the first warning, it will be someone you met or touched in the last twenty-four hours." He shook his head. "Can you imagine how rare a situation like that would be? Remember, preventable deaths don't happen all that often. You won't be saving people who die of disease or natural causes. You'll be saving people who would otherwise be killed by their actions or the actions of someone else. I know it sounds confusing right now, but as we get into the history a bit more, you'll understand it better.

"For now, know that I've touched tens, or even hundreds of thousands of people and I still go days and weeks without visions. Sometimes even months. In those rare instances when there is no vision beforehand, you need to just do the best you can. I won't lie to you, Dean. Those instances, as uncommon as they are, rarely end well."

I swallowed hard. "I think I just need time to let this soak in a bit. It still feels like it's not real sometimes."

Archer smiled. "Don't expect that feeling to ever fully go away."

"Where did the Society come from?" Lisa asked.

"We don't have time for a full history lesson," Archer said, "and even if we did, there is some debate on the topic. What we generally agree on is that it started more than a thousand years ago during a time when kings were quick to war and failed to value human lives the way they should've. The Society has had to evolve, but it very much follows the premise it was founded on: life is worth saving."

Colin's eyes widened. "It started in a time when there were kings?"

"There are still kings today, you idiot," Lisa said. Their ensuing argument fell into the background and mixed with the patter of rain and traffic sounds from the streets around the park.

A single question had worked my mind like a jackhammer ever since the mugging that changed my life— ever since I interrupted the back-alley attack on Mr. Vidmar. At first I'd thought about the question with resentment, but not now. My sister would've been killed by a BMW, and Mr. Cosler would've been killed by his funnel cake if we hadn't intervened. Still, the question remained, but it was with fear that I asked it. Fear that I wouldn't like the answer, or that it would put terrible pressure on me. My eyes locked with Archer, and he lifted an eyebrow. I stepped forward, hesitating for a minute before I spoke.

"Why me?" I asked finally.

Lisa and Colin stopped fighting and turned their attention to Archer. They'd probably wondered the same thing.

Archer contemplated the sky. The rain splattered against the side of the truck. After long seconds, he turned back to me. "I'd like to give you an answer, Dean. But the truth is I really don't know why you were chosen. We've gone back and forth about that at the Society. Everyone has an opinion. Maybe it was because you helped Vidmar. Maybe he saw something in you. Or maybe he'd been so badly beaten that he didn't realize what he was doing."

"You think he made a mistake?" The words fell out of my mouth before I realized I was speaking, and I felt my face warm at having exposed my insecurity.

"No," Archer said without pause. "Not at all. You tried to save your neighbor, and you actually saved your sister and that guy at the mall..."

"Arnold Cosler," Colin said.

Archer pointed at Colin and nodded. "Arnold Cosler, right, he'd be dead right now if you three hadn't intervened." He shook his head. "No, Dean, there isn't a person in the Society who won't welcome you. You're the right kid to have the gift, but I've no idea how Vidmar knew that." He drummed his fingers in time with the rain.

"Did he have to give it to me?" I asked. "I mean, did he have to give it to someone before he died? Is that one of the rules or something?"

Archer shook his head. "It was his gift to give. There aren't any rules about it. But we have a process for vetting and training people who might be good for the Society. A process that prepares them for what they'll experience."

"Why not just give it to everyone?" Lisa asked. "Wouldn't the world be a better place if everyone had it?"

Archer shook his head. "Even if that were possible—

and it's not—it wouldn't be a good idea. People aren't all the same, Lisa. Some people would use the gift for their own benefit. Others would just go insane with the visions or the failures. It would be cruel to give it to just anyone. It should be a choice." He looked back at me. "It should've been a choice for you too. It was a choice for me, one I almost didn't make. And I've seen dozens of people go through the training only to turn down the gift in the end. It's not an easy way to live."

"Do you ever regret it?" I asked.

"Accepting the gift?" Archer asked. "There are moments when I feel like maybe I'm not the best person for this. But I've saved a lot of people, Dean. I don't regret accepting it. At least, I haven't yet."

"So no one is going to take it away from him?" Colin asked. "Because he's too young or something?"

"They couldn't even if they wanted to," Archer answered.

In a blink, my chest warmed with relief, and at the same time my stomach knotted with fear. Somewhere in the back of my mind, I'd expected there to be a way to remove the gift if I decided I didn't want it. But suddenly I realized that I did want it, no matter how hard or strange it would make my life.

A thunderous boom directly overhead made me jump, and the rain became fat drops. We were getting drenched, and rain was pounding the side of the ice cream truck, soaking Archer and the stuff just inside the opening on the side.

"Tell the police," Archer said, raising his voice above the downpour. "Don't get between the robbers and the guards, just tell the police. Remember, changing one little thing, like increasing patrols in an area, is usually enough."

"Wait," Colin said. "That's it? We still have questions. When does Dean get his gear?"

"Gear?"

"You know, like his grappling hooks, tiny cameras, and exploding pens. That sort of stuff."

Archer laughed but ignored the question. "I'd invite you three into the truck, but inviting kids into an ice cream truck is a bit creepier than just leaving them to get soaked." He lifted a board that would fill the hole in the side of the truck. "Don't worry, I'll see you again. Good luck with the police." He slid the wood in place, and a second later, the truck roared to life and pulled away.

"He's a bit weird," Lisa said.

"I like him," Colin said. "He reminds me of James Bond."

"Oh yeah, they both drive really hot cars," Lisa said.

"Ha, ha." Colin turned to me. "What do you think, Dean?"

I blinked twice and wiped rain off my face. "I think we're about to lie to the police."

CHAPTER 18

The police station smelled like potpourri, which I wasn't expecting. I thought it would smell like criminals, and in my mind, criminals smelled like a mixture of smoke, sweat, and booze. Maybe the station smelled like that when the potpourri ran out. Each step I took toward the information counter tightened the knot in my stomach. *This has to work*, I told myself. *It has to.*

The officer behind the desk had a pale, narrow face and brown hair thin enough to see his scalp. He raised his chin when we walked up and said tiredly, "If you kids are just trying to get out of the rain, this isn't the place."

Our soaking clothes stuck to our bodies like colorful second skins. Lisa swiped a few wet strands of hair out of her eyes, and Colin just stood there, dripping. I glanced back at the muddy prints we'd tracked from the door and grimaced. We'd discussed how this was going to work while we walked to the police station: what we had to say, what we'd probably be asked, how we'd respond. I'd been concentrating on not messing it up to the point that I almost forgot how soaked we were. I wished we'd had more time to think things through. Another crack of thunder yanked me from my daze, and I turned back to the officer.

"We'd like to report a robbery." I wanted to sound grown-up, but my voice came out several octaves deeper than I was going for and just made me sound like an idiot.

The officer didn't seem to notice. "You've been robbed?"

"No," Lisa said. "We heard someone talking about robbing a place, and we'd like to report it."

"I see." The officer pushed his fingers through what little hair he had and tapped the keys on his computer. Then he snatched up the phone on his right, waited a moment, and said, "Detective Peters? I've got a couple kids up here who want to report a robbery. Uh-huh. Okay." He replaced the phone and gestured to bench. "Take a seat."

"But... couldn't we just tell you what we heard and leave it at that?" I asked. The plan was to keep it simple.

"That's not how it works," the officer said. Colin and Lisa both opened their mouths to speak, but the officer just pointed to the benches again. "Have a seat."

"This was supposed to be quick," Colin muttered as we took our seats. "Just in and out."

"We should've just called it in," Lisa whispered.

I shook my head. "We already discussed this. Cops probably get a million prank calls a day, and this is too important. If they thought we were just kids playing a gag, then what?" I didn't give them a chance to answer. "Two people will die, that's what." I shook my head again. "We have to make sure they believe us. I need to *know* they're going to do something. If we made an anonymous call, we wouldn't know if they took it seriously."

Lisa bit her lip. "You're right." She lowered her voice and leaned past Colin. "But we could get in a lot of trouble for this."

Colin fidgeted with his cell phone, then stuffed it in his pocket and wiped his palms across his jeans. I couldn't tell if he was excited or scared, but I suspected he was a little of both. He was usually the confident one, but I think he knew as well as I did that this wasn't some innocent prank we were pulling off. It was serious. Deadly serious.

We're saving lives, I reminded myself. *Pull it together.*

I'd barely finished my thought when the door to the left of the information counter swung open and a short, slender woman with dark hair and a gun on her hip stepped out. She had dark pants and a blue dress shirt that reminded me of what my mom sometimes wore to work—minus the gun, of course. We stared at her for several long seconds until she glanced at us and then turned to the officer at the information counter, who gave an uninterested flick of his head in our general direction. We stood up as she approached.

The detective had a face as smooth as polished steel,

and she looked at least as tough. She narrowed her dark eyes and tilted her head as she drew near and studied us the way my mom studied abstract paintings. She wore the look of a skeptic, the kind of look you'd expect from someone who has been lied to for most of her life. My high school principal had that same look.

"I'm Detective Peters," she said, reaching out her hand.

"I'm Lisa Green," Lisa said, shaking the detective's hand.

"I'm C—Colin," Colin said, shivering. "Colin Blane."

When she turned to me, I froze and stared at her outstretched hand. I was reminded yet again that if I touched her hand, I'd be inexorably linked to her. Police officers were pretty high on my list of people not to touch. They got shot at every day, plus they were always going into dangerous places and fighting dangerous people. The only profession higher on my list of people to avoid was soldiers. Visions of officers or soldiers getting killed would probably be a special kind of horror, and what can you do to stop someone going to war? Not much, that was for sure. I wasn't about to link myself to this lady.

I brought my hand to my mouth and coughed. "I'm Dean." I held up my palms. "I'd shake your hand, but I think I'm coming down with something." I felt a twinge of guilt for not touching her hand. I wondered if maybe I was being selfish. What would Archer think if he knew I was trying not to touch people? Would he care? Would he think I was a coward?

The officer shrugged, then eyed us carefully. "So, you three know something about a robbery?"

"That's right," I said. I took a second to consider the lie, or half lie, that we'd created on the way over. "We were—"

Detective Peters held up her hand. "C'mon back."

"Back?" Colin asked.

"That's right," she said, pulling open the door and standing to the side. "Through here. I'll take your statement."

CHAPTER 19

Detective Peters led us down a narrow hallway and through another door that opened into a large room humming with activity. A few dozen desks filled the area, and police officers moved between them like marching ants. The detective herded us to an empty workstation, pulled two empty chairs from neighboring desks, and told us to sit. She typed some stuff into her computer, then turned back to us and stared, unblinking, for what seemed like several minutes.

"Tell me about this robbery," she said finally.

Lisa spoke first and kept to the script we'd worked out. "We heard two guys talking outside the museum. They said they were going to break into the place tonight."

The officer remained stone-faced. "There were two of them?"

"Yes, ma'am," I said, doing my best to sound confident.

"And all three of you heard them?"

"Yes, ma'am," the three of us said together.

"And they said they'd be breaking into the museum?"

We nodded.

She turned to Colin. "What did they look like?"

"Oh, we didn't see them," Lisa said, answering for him. "They were behind some bushes."

"But we heard them," I added quickly. "Clear as a bell. There was no mistaking what they said. Plus, they sounded dangerous."

"They *sounded* dangerous?"

I swallowed. That part wasn't part of the plan, and I could see the muscles in Lisa's face clench. She was worried, no doubt, that I'd gone off script. I hadn't intended to say that, but the detective didn't seem as interested as I'd imagined. The last thing I wanted was for Detective Peters to think we were lying or had heard wrong. She eyed me with obvious suspicion.

"They sounded dangerous to me. You know, hushed tones, all serious."

"*Hushed* tones?" she asked. "But you said, just a second ago, that they were speaking clear as a bell."

Lisa's whole body stiffened, and Colin shifted uncomfortably on his chair. I felt beads of sweat form on my forehead. It was time for me to shut up or I was going to ruin everything. "I'm not sure what I mean," I said. "We did hear them clearly and maybe it was just the way they spoke that sounded dangerous."

She turned to Colin. "Tell me how you knew there were two of them?"

"Um, well, we heard two voices," Colin said.

"But you didn't see them at all?" Her expression remained the same, but I could hear in her tone she wasn't buying it.

"The bushes were really thick," Lisa offered.

The officer drew in a deep breath and let it out slowly. "Look, you three seem like good kids. I know you might think it's funny to play a prank." Her eyes met mine. "Maybe get some revenge on a museum for kicking you out?"

"W—What?" I asked.

She raised her brows. "Did you think I wouldn't recognize you from the paper, Mr. Curse? You've been in it a few times, you know. Plus, I'm not about to forget a story about the boy who took down a monk."

"We're not lying," Colin said, raising his hand like he was swearing on a stack of Bibles.

"Okay, Colin," she said, nodding. "You heard two men talking about robbing a museum. Two men, only a few feet away, just beyond some bushes, and you expect me to believe that you didn't even peek to see who they were?"

"N—No," Colin stammered. "I mean, um, yes." He cleared his throat and tugged at the collar of his wet shirt.

"Which is it?" Her voice hardened.

This was not how this was supposed to go. We'd talked through all the possible questions the police might ask us, but her not believing us so quickly caught us off guard. Of course it looked like I was just getting revenge on the museum. I should have realized that. I could've kicked myself for being so stupid.

Colin turned to me then glanced around the room, frantic for someone, anyone, to rescue him.

"I've been a detective a long time, Colin," Peters continued. "I know witnesses. I also have five older brothers and three kids of my own. Sons." She said the word *sons* like she was saying the name of a great battle. "You remind me of one of my brothers, and he wasn't the kind of kid who would hear two men planning a heist and not peek. You still expect me to believe that you just walked away without a glance?"

She was right. Colin would have hopped the fence to try to shake their hands. Real live robbers. He would have treated them like movie stars. He probably would've asked them for autographs.

Lisa and I opened our mouths to speak, but the detective pointed at us and spoke without taking her eyes off Colin. "You two don't speak. Not a word. I'm talking to Mr. Blane for a moment." Her gaze narrowed on Colin. "Well?"

In my head, I begged Colin not to mess it up. Just say you didn't look. Just say you couldn't wait to get away from there, find the police to report it.

"I... I, um, might have peeked," Colin said. I slapped

my forehead. The detective glanced at me with an expression that screamed "Gotcha!"

"No, you didn't," Lisa interjected.

I groaned. We hadn't talked about what the people could have looked like because we had agreed we weren't going to give descriptions. Colin tugged at his collar and rubbed the back of his neck. He looked more nervous than I'd ever seen him.

"Ms. Green, I won't ask you to be quiet again." She turned back to Colin. "What did they look like?"

Colin's gaze darted around the room again, flitting from one place to another, never fully settling on any one thing. Then he turned back, and in a rush of words that seemed to fall from his mouth, said, "One of them had brown hair, a mustache, and a green windbreaker."

"And the other one?" Peters raised one brow.

The next description came just as fast, like he didn't like the taste of the words and wanted them out of his mouth immediately. "The other one was black, about six feet tall, with really short hair and a goatee. He was wearing dress pants and a white button-up shirt."

I sighed. Not bad, Colin. A button-up shirt wasn't very burglar-like, but that's not a bad thing. Colin wasn't usually such a quick thinker. Actually, he wasn't much of a thinker at all. I hoped our interrogator would buy the descriptions.

Peters glanced over her shoulder, then back to Colin

and then to me and Lisa. "Do you guys agree? Is that what they looked like?"

What could we do? If we said no, then we would make Colin a liar, but if we said yes, maybe they'd go out and round up everyone who matched that description. But as long as they believed us, they'd have to go to the museum. They'd have to increase patrols, and besides, Colin's description seemed pretty believable to me.

"Yes," I said, "that's what we saw." Lisa nodded, hesitantly, in agreement.

"Hanson. Mitchell," Detective Peters called over her shoulder. "Could you guys come over here for a second?"

I groaned when the two men stepped up. "Colin, you idiot," I muttered. Officer Hanson and Officer Mitchell were identical to the two men Colin had just described, right down to the windbreaker and goatee. If it wouldn't have made me look nuts (or more nuts), I would have stood up and punched Colin right then and there. Not that I would have done a lot better, I supposed. I felt my face flush, and Lisa lowered her chin.

"What's up, Peters?" the officer in the green windbreaker asked.

"Oh, I'm just wondering if you two are planning on robbing the museum later this evening."

"Um, no," the officer with the goatee said. "But plans can change. Do you want me to let you know if we change our minds and decide to steal some dinosaur bones later on?"

"Yes, please," Peters replied. "Thanks, guys, that'll be all."

The two officers turned and walked away snickering. Great.

"Let me guess," she said, glaring at Colin. "The men you saw and those two officers shop at the same place?"

Colin stammered for a couple seconds, a series of random syllables that made him, and, by association, us, seem completely out of touch with sanity. The detective looked each of us, one by one, directly in the eye.

When her gaze settled on me, I gulped and gripped the armrest on my chair. Maybe if I explained, not the whole truth, but enough for her to know we weren't making it up... I tried to work out what I could say in my head, but everything seemed to end with the Society being compromised. "We didn't actually see any—"

"Don't," Peters warned, her slender finger pointing at my face. "You helped that Russian fellow who was getting mugged, and then the three of you tried to help your neighbor not too long ago, so I know you're good kids. But I've been doing this job a while, and I'm pretty good at telling when people are lying. You guys are the worst liars I've seen in a while." Her eyes narrowed. "You didn't overhear anyone planning a robbery, did you?"

Her words scratched me like sharp branches. She was right: we were lying. And it was ruining the whole thing. Not that the truth would have been any better, but maybe if Colin hadn't bungled it with his stupid descriptions, or if I hadn't messed up and put her on edge in the first place, things would have gone a bit better.

"Here's what I'm going to do," Peters said. "I'm going to give you just ten seconds to walk back the way you came and I'll forget this ever happened. I won't say a couple kids tried to file a false police report; I won't call your parents. It'll be just between you and me. Ten seconds."

"Sounds good," Colin said.

He and Lisa stood and turned for the door. But I couldn't move. I couldn't just walk away from this. I leaned forward. "Please, Detective Peters, could you just have a patrol car drive around the museum at..." I paused, if the deaths were supposed to happen at 12:40, the actual break-in would be at least ten minutes earlier—or maybe fifteen? How long did it take to break in, get caught, and kill someone? I took a guess. "Around 12:25? Just have a car loop the block at that time, please?"

Her mouth became a thin line, and she stared hard at me for several seconds. "Ten, nine, eight, seven..."

Colin heaved me to my feet and dragged me through the door we had come through, down the corridor, across the lobby, and out the main entrance before our seconds expired. None of us seemed to care that the rain hadn't let up or that we were drenched again. We just lowered our heads and slogged our way to the bus stop.

Silently.

CHAPTER 20

The bus pulled up about fifteen minutes after we made it to the stop. By then, we were no less drenched than if we'd just crawled out of a pool. I collapsed onto a seat at the back and dropped my head into my hands.

"I'm sorry, guys," Colin said after the bus lurched forward. They were the first words any of us had spoken since we'd left the precinct, and it just made frustration flare in my chest. Colin added, "I just didn't expect someone so small to be so intimidating. I got flustered and then I just—"

"We know what you did," I snapped. Colin stared at the floor.

"It's not all his fault, Dean," Lisa said, "and you know it." I couldn't remember the last time Lisa had come to Colin's defense, and given how Colin looked up suddenly, I bet he was just as confused.

"What do you mean it wasn't all his fault?" I asked. "Of course it was."

"It *was* my fault," Colin agreed.

"It wasn't *totally* your fault," Lisa said sternly. "But

you are an idiot for giving a cop's description to another cop. I mean, what the heck were you thinking?" Colin shrugged, and Lisa added, "It really doesn't matter, though. That cop wasn't buying our story from the minute we walked in there."

"She might still send a car," Colin said. "She might. And if she does, that might be all we need to stop the robbers."

"Sure, Colin," Lisa said. "That's not wishful thinking at all." She lowered her voice and muttered, "We'll have to call Archer."

"Archer." I groaned. "Great. We've been part of the Society for, like, a day and already we have to call and say we couldn't do it on our own." Several long seconds passed, and when I looked up, Colin was grinning. "What?" I asked.

"You said we." His smile widened. "You said 'We've been part of the Society for a day,' not just you've been part of it. Thanks. I thought that maybe with my screw-up back there you might not want me to... you know..."

"Yeah, well, we'll see if you're still thanking me when we're trying to stop some burglars and security guards from killing each other tonight." That made Colin laugh, but it made a fist-sized knot form behind my ribs. Still, I forced a smile and jabbed Colin's shoulder.

Lisa rolled her eyes. "Are you guys going to kiss or

something? Because if you're all done making up, we better make that call." She fished her cell out of her purse and held it out. Water beaded off the surface, and the display, or at least parts of it, flickered like it was having a seizure. She blinked and gasped. "Oh no. It got soaked in the rain. My parents are going to kill me!"

I pulled mine out of my pocket and it was just was wet as Lisa's, and just as broken. "Mine too," I said, groaning.

Colin smirked. "I'm not sure if you can have visions of yourself, but at least if Lisa's parents are going to kill her, you can give her the heads up twenty-four hours before they do."

I cringed a bit at the thought of seeing one of my friends in a vision. Colin pulled his cell phone out of his pocket and held it up. It was just as wet as mine and Lisa's, but the display was clear. "They do make waterproof phones, you know." He pressed the speed dial and handed it to me.

I called Archer six times and left two messages before the bus arrived at our stop. Lisa stopped me when I tried to call for the seventh time; she said I was going to scare him off. I was pretty sure you couldn't scare someone who had the same kind of visions as me, but I decided not to push it.

"Where is he?" I wondered out loud.

"He'll get your messages," Lisa said. "Don't worry." Her voice shook, and I was pretty sure she was just as worried as I was. We trudged down the puddled sidewalk. The rain had eased from a torrent into a sprinkle that I barely felt because I was already so wet.

"We can't just wait for him," Colin said. "We can't just hope he gets the message or that he's going to handle it for us. Remember what he said? How we're supposed to handle things on our own?"

"Not something like this," Lisa insisted. "He told us to call him if it didn't go well at the police station. I'd say it didn't go very well."

"Fine," Colin snapped, "we called him. Do you really want to just sit around and wait to see if everything works out?"

"Colin's right," I said before Lisa could argue back. "We have to do something." Our options were pretty limited. We had tried the police, and we'd called Archer. That left only one option that I could see, and by the way Lisa was chewing her lip and Colin was nodding, they knew what I was going to say. "We'll have to go there."

"Unless Archer calls," Lisa said.

"Unless Archer calls," I agreed.

After a few more minutes, Colin said, "It won't be that

tough, guys. All we have to do is sneak out, bike down to that little park across from the museum, and just call the police if we see anything."

"And why didn't we just do that in the first place?" Lisa asked sarcastically. "Oh, yeah, because last time we did that, Dean's neighbor got killed."

"This is different," Colin said.

"He's right," I said. "What else can we do?"

"The guards have real guns, Dean," Lisa said. "Guns that shoot real bullets. I don't want to get shot."

"None of us *want* to get shot," Colin said.

"We'll stay in the park," I said. "We'll do what Colin said and call the police as soon as we see anything suspicious. The police department isn't so far away from the museum; it'll take them, like, two minutes to get there."

"We won't leave that little park?" Lisa asked. "Not for anything?"

"Not for anything," I said.

She turned to Colin, who put his hand on his heart and smiled. "Not for anything," he said. "It'll be easy. Remember, Detective Peters might make police patrol the area anyway, so the robbers might not even show up." He turned and muttered, "But I wouldn't count on that."

"We'll have to sneak out around midnight," I said. I pointed at a small gathering of trees a dozen or so meters from where we were standing. "Let's just meet right there at midnight. It won't take long to bike down there." I scratched my chin.

Lisa pointed at Colin. "Don't forget your phone."

"Yeah, yeah, don't worry, I won't." He rubbed his hands together and smiled. "C'mon, guys, this is great. It's happening. Show some enthusiasm. We're going to save some people tonight. Aren't you excited?"

Lisa and I looked at each other, then back to Colin, and we both answered at the same time.

"No."

CHAPTER 21

Mr. Overton had called from the museum to tell my mom that he appreciated my apology, so when I got home my parents were in a good mood.

"He said he wouldn't let Sok back into the museum," I said during dinner.

"Sock?" Becky asked. She turned to my mom. "He just called that monk a sock?"

I rolled my eyes. "It's S-O-K, and it's his name, genius."

"At least you tried, Dean." My mom smiled. "I'm very proud of you."

"Me too," my dad said. "It was very grown up of you, Dean."

"Yeah, you're a real big boy now," Becky chimed in. She clapped her hands and added, "Maybe you'll stop asking to sleep in Mom and Dad's room now."

"At least I don't play with pieces of poop," I said.

"Gah!" Becky yelled. "How many times do I have to tell you that they're fossils? Fossils are like stones. They're perfectly clean to touch."

My dad chuckled. I think sometimes he liked it when

Becky and I fought. Like maybe he thought we were a couple of test subjects in an experiment on sibling rivalry or something. Or maybe there was a book out there in psychotherapy land that said it was healthy when brothers and sisters fought. I wondered if he'd think it was healthy if I tied my sister up and tossed her in a closet.

I spent the rest of the night trying to look innocent, which wasn't easy because my nerves made me jump every time someone spoke to me, and I had a constant feeling of nausea that would only let up if I kept moving. As a result, I paced every room in the house. Becky said it looked like I had to pee and kept asking me if I was wearing my special rubber underwear. When Becky turned on some modern-day princess movie later in the evening, I pretended to be annoyed and said I was going to bed. I pulled on a pair of dark jeans and a black, long-sleeved shirt, pulled the covers up to my chin, and waited.

It wasn't the first time I'd snuck out of the house at night, but it was the first time I'd done it so early. By eleven o'clock, most of the house was silent. My parents often read in bed, and if I listened carefully, I thought I could hear them talking. I waited another forty-five minutes, during which I tried my best not to move an inch. It was the longest forty-five minutes of my life.

A few minutes before midnight, I slid out of my covers and positioned my pillow and some clothing under my blankets to make it look like I was still there. I slipped on my shoes and climbed onto the roof.

Even though it had stopped raining shortly after dinner, the shingles were still slick. I had to crawl to the edge. Just below the rain gutter was a wall of lattice that rose up behind my mom's small flowerbed. It used to be covered with this big climbing vine, but my dad chopped the vine out when it started taking root in the side of the house and cracking the mortar. The lattice was as easy to climb down as a ladder.

As soon as my feet hit dirt, I grabbed my bike and raced to the meeting spot.

Colin was already waiting, which didn't surprise me at all. His room was on the first floor of his house, so he just had to jump out of a window. Also, his parents were the soundest sleepers in the world. A couple years ago, he had a sleepover at his house with at least a dozen guys from school. We played video games all night long, and no matter how loud we got, we could hear Colin's dad snoring upstairs. I figured his mom must sleep with earplugs or something. Colin could probably sneak out wearing drums as shoes and not get caught.

"Where's Lisa?" I asked.

He shook his head. "She sent an email. Her parents are still awake. She can't get out. I told her I'd text her when we got there."

"Darn it," I muttered, and then asked, "Did you hear from Archer?" I knew the answer. If Colin had heard from Archer, he'd have called me right away. Still, I had to ask.

He shook his head. "You know I haven't."

"Why didn't he call back?" I asked.

"Oh, relax, Dean, it's going to be fine. The plan's so simple it's almost not even a plan." He smiled, full of confidence. "We're just going to call the police if the burglars show up." He grabbed a backpack from the ground and threw it over his shoulder. "C'mon, let's go."

"Wait, what's in the bag?" I asked.

"Just stuff we might need. I'll show you when we get there."

Stuff we might need could be anything in Colin's world. His imagination was so unpredictable that he might have had a live animal in there with a perfectly reasonable (in his mind) explanation for why it was necessary and how it could be used. I decided not to push it and climbed on my bike.

We kept to the alleys and side streets, riding as hard as we could. It took us fifteen minutes to get to the park. Colin didn't slow down and biked straight through the gate. I was right behind him. There was a shout of pain, and I'd barely squeezed the brakes when my bike hit a mass on the ground and I went over the handlebars.

Colin and I disentangled ourselves from our bikes, and the soft thing we'd hit jumped up. A homeless man, who must have been sleeping near the gate, was on his feet with a clear bike tread painted in mud across his tattered gray hoodie. He shouted some slurred curses that I couldn't understand and staggered to the back of the playground, into the shadows.

I brushed myself off and whispered, "Got anything in your little bag to get rid of *him*?"

"No," Colin said, gazing in the direction the man had gone. "I have some firecrackers. Maybe we can scare him off with them or something."

"You don't really have firecrackers in there, do you?"

He smirked. "Next time I'll bring something for him. A sandwich, maybe."

"A sandwich?" I asked. "And what do you mean next time? There better not be a next time."

I peeked over the bushes. The museum was dimly lit and looked completely vacant. There might have been guards roaming around in there, but there weren't any out front. "The front," I said out loud, realizing our mistake. "How could we be so stupid?"

"Huh?" Colin said, looking over my shoulder.

"What if the burglars come from the back? We won't

even see them. And if it is Sok robbing the place, he might come from the back because that's where the Buddha head is on display."

"I thought you said you didn't think it was Sok," Colin said.

I shook my head. "No, I said there are a lot of valuable things in the museum, and it could be anyone going after almost anything."

"It doesn't matter because I got us covered." Colin smiled, then hunched and unzipped his bag. He pulled out a couple of walkie-talkies and handed one to me. "I wasn't sure if we'd need these things, but I thought we might. I'll go around back since you're still kinda slow with that leg of yours."

"My leg's fine," I said. Though I realized I did kind of favor it when I walked, and Colin was a bit faster than me anyway.

He shook his head. "If the robbers spot us, we'll have to run. I'll call the police if I see anything, and if you see anything over here, just tell me and I'll call 9-1-1."

I glanced into the open bag and caught a glimpse of rope and several rolls of duct tape. I was going to ask if he was planning on kidnapping someone and tying them to a chair, but decided not to waste any more time listening to Colin's explanations. "Wait," I said, "what if that homeless guy comes back?"

Colin shrugged. "I dunno. Strike up a conversation. Ask him what his hobbies are." He checked his watch. "Are you ready? It's already twenty after twelve. I better get back there. You said someone dies around 12:40, right? So they could get here any second. They might already be here." He didn't wait for me to answer any of his questions. Instead he jumped onto his bike and pedaled through the gate. I watched him disappear around the block.

"Ask him what his hobbies are?" I muttered. "That's what I should do if the crazy homeless guy comes back to kill me? Thanks, Colin, real helpful." I would have preferred if he'd given me a can of bear spray or something. I glanced nervously at the shadows and shivered as I imagined the homeless man poised to pounce.

I complained to myself for a couple more minutes and even had time to wonder if I would have visions of myself if I was going to die. Then a gray moving truck pulled up and backed slowly into the narrow alley between the museum and the bakery.

"Colin," I said into the walkie-talkie. "There's a truck over here, get ready." I thought it was weird that Colin didn't answer, but imagined him poised with his phone in one hand, walkie-talkie in the other, just waiting for the word.

It could be a delivery truck, I told myself. It could be a delivery truck for the bakery. Or maybe it was a truck dropping off something. *It could be anything*, I told myself. *Maybe it's—*

Something caught my eye on the roof of the truck, and it wasn't until I blinked twice that I saw two figures, dressed in black—just like the figure in my vision—pull themselves onto the top of the truck and jump to the museum's roof.

CHAPTER 22

"Call the police. Call the police!" I whispered forcefully into the walkie-talkie.

Garbled words punctuated with static responded to my message.

"Colin? Did you get that? Colin?"

I cursed myself for not testing the thing before Colin left—or for letting Colin leave in the first place. If he'd heard me, the police could be on their way, but if he was only getting static and half of every third word, he wouldn't have a clue what I was saying.

"Colin!" I said again, more desperate this time. "Call the police."

Nothing.

One of the robbers pressed himself against the wall of the second floor and peered at the street below while the other one crept across the roof. Then the first robber hunched and seemed to be struggling with something. There must be a way in up there, I decided, a hatch maybe. I imagined them crawling through a heating vent and dropping down into a massive gunfight where everyone died. I couldn't let that happen. I ran to the gate, intending to shout at them in hopes of scaring them off, but instead I stepped on something round and hard and rolled my ankle, stumbling against the fence. When I looked up, the thieves were gone.

I tried the walkie-talkie again. This time I wasn't whispering. "Colin, you dolt, they're inside. Call the police!"

I plucked a fist-sized stone from the grass—probably the very one I'd just rolled my ankle on—and rushed into the street. I was acting on impulse now. "Hey!" I shouted. "Hey, I see you up there!" I didn't see them. I knew they were already making their way into the building.

I cocked my arm and was about to throw the rock at the roof, hoping that maybe luck or some divine intervention would direct the stone through the hatch the robbers had used, or at least create enough of a clatter to make them turn back.

Then I decided it wouldn't work. I'd be lucky to get the stone onto the roof. I adjusted my aim and focused on the large glass windows at the front of the building and threw with everything I had.

Someone yelled, "No! Don't!" from my right, just as the rock left my hand. Half a second later, I was tackled off the curb and onto the street. There was the familiar sound of shattering glass, and a second thereafter, a strident alarm sliced the air around me.

I lay on the pavement and blinked, hoping the stars would stop swirling. The guy who'd tackled me pushed himself to his feet. He wore a dark jacket and a black ski mask, just like in my vision. "What did you do?" he asked in a familiar accent.

"Sok?" I asked. "It is you, isn't it?"

He growled and brought his hands behind his head and then turned back to the museum. "You ruined everything," he muttered.

I staggered to my feet and quickly grabbed the top of his hood and pulled. The fabric came off like a Band-Aid. "I knew it!" I said.

Sok looked dumbly back at first, and then glared frozen daggers at me. "What are you doing here?" he spat. "This could've been over. Why'd you have to get involved?"

"You're mad at me? You're the one breaking—" Before I could really tell him off, the truck in the alley roared to life. Sok spun around and sprinted away, throwing himself into the cab before it sped around the corner. Shouts carried over the sirens from inside the museum, and I scrambled across the street back to the park and dove through the gate. I risked a glance through the bushes just long enough to see a security guard stepping through the broken window, shining his flashlight one way, then the next. A police car, lights flashing, screeched around the corner.

"Colin," I muttered. He was somewhere on the other

side of the building. I hoped he'd had the good sense to run when the alarms went off. Who was I kidding? Knowing him, he'd probably found a way into the museum and was hanging out in one of the displays, completely oblivious to everything.

Another police car raced down the street and skidded to a stop in front of the museum. The blue and amber lights painted the leaves on the trees and bushes like Christmas ornaments. I spun around to grab my bike and nearly jumped out of my skin. My bike was where I'd left it, but it wasn't alone. The homeless man was crouched beside it, stroking the seat and handlebars like the bike was some kind of wheeled pet.

"Um, sir?" I whispered, "I really need my bike."

The man jerked around and bared his teeth like a mother bear protecting her cub.

"Whoa!" I said, still hushed. "Okay, okay, look." I held out Colin's useless walkie-talkie. "I'll trade you. The bike for this, um, this super cool..." The voices from over the fence seemed louder, like someone was coming over to check out the park. While I was distracted, the homeless bicycle fanatic lunged out and snatched the walkie-talkie from my hand.

"Oh, c'mon, man," I begged. "Just give me back my bike." I risked a step closer, and the crazy hobo reached into the ripped pocket of his jacket and pulled out a long, narrow object that, at first glance, looked a lot like a knife. He lunged forward and grabbed me by the collar with his empty hand and then shoved me away. I stumbled backwards but managed to stay on my feet. A flash of light illuminated his hand. I saw what he was holding: a toothbrush.

"Back," he growled, brandishing his weapon like some crazed dentist.

The toothbrush was silver, which I figured was why it looked like a blade. It had flattened bristles that were as brown as the man's teeth. I wasn't afraid that he'd try to stab me with it, but I was kind of worried that he might try to brush my teeth with it.

A radio crackled through the bushes. I didn't have time for this. Even if I somehow managed to wrestle my bike away from him, I'd never get it over the fence before the cops saw me. I turned, sprinted across the grass, and threw myself over the fence into the narrow alley behind the park. I landed in a heap on broken pavement but kept my mouth firmly closed. I hadn't had a chance to move before I heard a female voice shout, "Don't move!" At first I thought she was yelling at me and I froze, but then she shouted, "He has a knife!"

She was talking about the homeless guy.

I stood up and was about to run when the very last thing I wanted to happen happened... everything around me turned gray.

CHAPTER 23

"No," I said under my breath. "No, it can't be happening." Sok wasn't anywhere around. I'd seen him get into the truck, and it was long gone by now. I jerked my head around one way, then the other, in the unlikely event that Sok or maybe that security guard had followed me into the alley. They hadn't. I checked my watch: 12:48. It was after the time the security guard was supposed to die.

Archer's words hammered my skull: "If you touch someone for the first time moments before they're going to die, you'll still be warned."

"The homeless guy," I said, remembering that he'd just shoved me moments earlier.

As if on cue, the policewoman shouted from across the bushes, "Put down your weapon!" She was talking about the toothbrush. He was probably just trying to protect his pet bike. The way I saw it, I had two options: find another rock and throw it at the police officer and hope I hit her (or the homeless guy), or scream like a crazy person and hope she didn't shoot anyone... especially me. Oh, and for both those options, I had to run as fast as I could, because no matter what happened, if I got caught, I'd be in a lot of trouble. Unless I was trying to hit a plate glass window, my aim sucked. I decided on option number two.

"It's not a knife!" I screamed. "It's just a toothbrush!" I poked my head through the bushes. "Don't shoot!"

A *bang* and a flash of light flared in the park. It sounded like an exploding stick of dynamite, and I'm embarrassed to admit it, but as soon as it happened, I started running. I didn't look back, and I didn't hesitate for a single step. I just surged forward. There were shouts behind me, but I'm not sure if they were directed at me or if they were just people shouting about the gunshot. I didn't wait around to find out.

Every cop in the area must've been at the playground, because I didn't even try to stay in the dark alleys or side streets. At one point, I was running right down the middle of a road, and I didn't see any police. I just ran as hard and as fast as I could, hoping that somehow I could outrun my thoughts, or that my pounding footsteps could silence the voice in my head shouting that the homeless man had just been shot, and it was my fault. I'd failed again. It was my bike he was trying to protect, and if I'd just taken the time to park it somewhere else, none of this would have happened.

I stopped twice because of cramps, and it was almost three o'clock in the morning when I made it back to my block. I slogged past the spot where I'd met Colin earlier, hoping he would be there. He wasn't. "I hope you got out of there, Colin," I said under my breath. I considered going by his house and knocking on his bedroom window, but I was too exhausted, and I could just as easily send him an email when I got home.

The neighborhood was still asleep when I turned onto my street. Every thought imaginable had entered my head on the long walk home. I imagined the police somehow tracing my bike back to me, or fingerprinting the rock I'd thrown through the picture window, and coming to my house to arrest me. Or maybe Detective Peters would remember those three kids who said there was going to be a break-in at the museum and think we were responsible.

Yet the houses were still dark and the street was utterly deserted. No one jumped out of the bushes to arrest me. No patrol cars were in my driveway. Nothing. As I climbed the lattice back up to the roof and crept through my bedroom window, I tried to feel good about what had happened. Colin and I had stopped a robbery. The security guard and Sok were both alive. It was a success. Except that I could still hear the gunshot, and every time I closed my eyes, I imagined the homeless man collapsed against the fence, a bullet hole in his chest. In my experience, when people shoot guns, someone always dies.

CHAPTER 24

I don't know how long it took me to get to sleep, but I woke up to someone poking me in the neck. I blinked twice and nearly peed my pants when I saw Becky's frizzy head a couple inches in front of my face. She clamped her hand over my mouth before I could yell and put a finger to her lips.

She took a couple deep breaths. "What are you into, Dean?" she whispered.

I rubbed my eyes and sat up. "What? Get out of my—"

"Shhhhh," she said, pressing her finger to her lips. Then she shook her head. She seemed really worried. It wasn't a look I'd seen a lot on Becky and it had a silencing effect on me.

She slapped a newspaper onto my legs. It was opened to a middle section and near the bottom of the page there was a small article with the title: *Seeking Three Angels*.

I rubbed the sleep out of my eyes and was about to read the article but Becky pulled it away. "It's about three kids who saved a guy at the mall." Her voice was still a whisper. "The guy wants to thank them."

I felt my eyes widen and I snatched the paper back and scanned the page. There wasn't any reference to me, Lisa, or Colin. Just some vague accounts by a couple people who thought they saw three kids helping a man with a peanut allergy.

I sighed and tossed the page back to Becky.

"It wasn't you?" she asked.

I swallowed. Last thing I needed was for Becky to run to my parents with this. I shook my head.

"Really? Because it happened the day Mom and I picked you and Lisa and Colin up from the mall."

"Becky," I said. "It wasn't me, okay? Now, why are you whispering?"

She nodded toward my bedroom door. "I don't know what you did. But there's a policewoman downstairs and she's talking to Mom and Dad about you."

I jumped out of bed. "Now?" I asked, frantic. "She's down there right now?"

"Shut up, you idiot," Becky whispered. "If they hear you, they'll call you downstairs. Mom or Dad will be up here any second. What the heck did you do anyway? Is it about what happened at the mall?"

"The mall? No... I, um, didn't do anything," I said. "Nothing. Nothing at all. I didn't do anything."

"Uh-huh," Becky said. "If they ask what you did, you might want to just say 'Nothing' once. When you say it a dozen times like that, you sound really guilty. And kind of crazy too."

She raised an eyebrow, stepped closer, and plucked something from my hair. "A leaf." She spun the stem between her fingers and waved her hand at me. "You look like you just went for a run in the woods." Before I could ask Becky what she wanted in exchange for her silence, she said something that surprised me. "If I were you, I'd jump in the shower, fast. And stop looking so... guilty. Jeez."

I grabbed clothes from the floor and sprinted, as silently as I could, for the bathroom. The whole time I was in the shower, all I could think was that maybe Colin had been captured, or maybe the homeless man had been killed. That, and my shoulder and back were killing me. I'd hit the pavement twice, and there was the beginning of a bruise on my arm and shoulder.

When I walked into the kitchen, I tried to do it innocently, but I'm sure I didn't look innocent at all. Detective Peters sat at the kitchen table with my mom and dad. She smiled when I walked in, but my mom spoke first.

"Dean." She looked like she was going to cry, and I wondered what they'd been talking about. "Apparently you know Detective Peters." It was one of those statements that might be a question so I wasn't sure how to respond. My mom didn't look angry—she looked hurt. I think she was really asking me why I hadn't told her about my visit with Detective Peters.

I nodded, and when I spoke, I concentrated on keeping my voice even despite my heart hammering against my ribs. "Good morning, Detective Peters."

"Good morning, Dean. I was just telling your mom and dad about our little meeting yesterday."

I blinked several times while I struggled for an appropriate response, one that wouldn't incriminate me but was still something a normal fourteen-year-old boy would say. These days, it was increasingly difficult to figure out what was and was not normal. "Did something happen at the museum?" I asked.

"Some vandalism," my dad said. Becky sidled into the kitchen and hovered by the sink. My dad cleared his throat and added, "Detective Peters said you might have overheard some people discussing a robbery."

I swallowed back my guilt and my desire to just come out and ask if the homeless man was okay. Had he been shot? Was he dead? But of course, if I asked that, they'd know I'd been there, and then I'd have even more explaining to do. I'd seen those police shows; I knew cops had special interrogation techniques and lie detector machines. If I wasn't careful, I could end up exposing the entire Society. I couldn't let that happen. I forced a laugh, but it came out sounding like a strangled goat.

"That's what it sounded like anyway," I managed.

"But after talking to Detective Peters yesterday, well, um, we figured we just didn't hear properly. And since it was just some vandalism, I guess you were right. Did you at least catch them?"

The detective tapped her lips and looked like she was trying to translate what I'd just said. "No." She shook her head. "There were some distractions. They got away."

I wanted to shout and give someone a high five. No one caught? No one? That meant Colin had gotten away. It also meant that the homeless man wasn't dead... didn't it? "That's too bad," I said, struggling to keep from smiling.

The detective cleared her throat. "Yesterday you said the people you heard sounded like adults?"

I nodded. "That's right."

My dad leaned over the counter and looked at me carefully. "A witness saw a kid running away from the museum last night."

I gasped. "What?" I shouldn't have been so surprised. It's not like I had tried to stay hidden. "Did they get a good look at him, um, or her?"

"No," Detective Peters answered. "But one of the officers on the scene swears she heard a young boy yell out at her. Is there any chance you might have heard kids, not adults?"

I shook my head.

"Is there anything else you remember, Dean?" my dad

asked. "Maybe you, um, recognized the voice or something? The witnesses didn't get a good look, but said it could have been a shorter adult or maybe a young boy." His voice changed to what Becky and I called his *therapist tone*. "Sometimes, when someone's been in the spotlight a lot, it might feel really good, and they might do things to make sure it doesn't end. So if you know someone that might apply to... a friend perhaps?"

My dad was obviously talking about me. I wondered how close the description of the fleeing kid had been. Did they know it had been me for sure? No. I decided quickly. If Detective Peters knew for sure, she wouldn't mess around. She seemed too tough for that. "I didn't recognize the voices," I said, working very hard not to sound guilty and resisting the urge to look at the floor. I read somewhere that liars always look at the floor.

My mom sobbed, and a tear rolled down her cheek.

"It wasn't me, Mom." I didn't want to lie, especially when my mom was already so emotional, but what choice did I have? There'd be too much explaining to do if I just told them the truth. Plus, if you belong to a secret society, lying is something you just have to get used to... right?

"Dean, no one said it was you. But if you wanted attention," my mom began, "or if you feel you need to act out to get some—"

"I don't want attention," I snapped. I looked at

Detective Peters. "I really don't want anything. I'm really sorry the place got vandalized. That's a real shame. But I've already told you everything."

The detective tilted her head. "Then you didn't sneak out last night?"

"W—What?" My voice squeaked, and I think I sounded like I was *trying* to sound shocked, rather than actually being shocked. My dad raised an eyebrow.

"Dean? Sneak out? Ha! Yeah, right." Becky laughed. She had her hands on her hips and scrunched her face. Detective Peters gave her a double look, which I wasn't sure if she did because of what my sister had said or because she noticed Becky's frizzy mop of hair. That hair is enough to make anyone do a double take—or triple for that matter.

"Sweetie," my dad said, "now's not the time to make fun of your brother."

Detective Peters nodded at Becky. "You don't think your brother would sneak out?"

"She doesn't think anything," I said. "She's allergic to thinking."

Becky's face flushed, and she glared at me for a few seconds and then turned back to the detective. "What I mean is that Dean's too much of a chicken to sneak out at night. Just the other day he was so afraid of the dark that he asked my parents if he could sleep in their room."

"Oh," Detective Peters said. The way she sai
me think she didn't believe Becky, which was good, but ..
still stopped her from following that line of questioning.

Any other time, I'd defend myself, but my sister's little
gibe actually seemed to make me look innocent, so I
decided to keep quiet. I gave Becky a sideways glance and
wondered if she had seen me sneak out, or maybe she'd
heard me sneak back in. I couldn't tell if she was helping
me or teasing me. It didn't matter.

"Okay, kids," my dad said. "That's enough." He
turned back to the detective. "Do you have any other
questions for my son?"

"No," she said, standing up from the table. "I think I
got what I came for. There were a lot of angry protestors at
the museum yesterday, and several of them were kids. The
vandals could be any of them."

Or none of them, I thought. I considered the gunshot
again, and the homeless man. Would Detective Peters be
so calm if someone had been shot? I was so full of nerves,
it felt like someone was taking a blender to my insides.

My parents walked her out, and as soon as the door
was closed, they turned and faced me.

"Dean," my dad said, "is there anything you want to
say to us?"

My mom grabbed a tissue from a table in the entrance
and blew her nose. "It wasn't you, was it, Dean? You

wouldn't do that, would you? And you're not protecting anyone, are you?"

I had a long morning ahead of me.

CHAPTER 25

It took another two hours of insisting I wasn't some out-of-control attention-seeker before my parents let me leave the house. "It's just an odd coincidence, Dean," my dad had said, "that, not long after you get kicked out of the museum, it gets vandalized."

In the end, they agreed with Detective Peters that it could have been any of the protestors. My mom kept asking me if I wanted a hug, and Becky kept sniggering from the back of the kitchen and mouthing the word "baby" over and over. I couldn't bring myself to get mad at her, though. Whether Becky had meant to or not, she'd helped convince the cop that I wasn't the culprit, even if Detective Peters now thought I was some blubbering wimp who slept with his mommy and daddy. I shuddered at that thought as I walked down the block.

Colin's house was huge—at least twice as big as my house, probably three times. It even had an iron gate at the front of the driveway, though I'd never actually seen it closed—not even at night. Colin didn't brag, or even talk about being rich, but he was.

"About time you got here!" Colin said when he came to the door. "Lisa's been here for half an hour already. What took you so long?" He grabbed me by the shoulder and pulled me into the house before I could answer and then shoved me across his tiled foyer and up the staircase.

"That detective came to my house first," Lisa said. "I tried to call you, but your mom said you were still sleeping."

"It's okay," I said. "It wasn't a big deal."

"Then they don't suspect us?" Colin asked.

I shook my head. "But what the heck happened to you last night? Why did it take you so long to call the cops?"

"My walkie-talkie wasn't working," he said. "Then as soon as the cops showed up, I took off. I figured you did the same. Except..."

"What?" I asked.

Lisa pursed her lips. "Colin said he heard a gunshot. I knew it wasn't true."

"I know what I heard," Colin said. He turned to me. "I actually thought I heard you shouting just before the shot. I thought you'd been killed, man. I even waited by the meeting place for an hour, hoping you'd stop by, but you never showed."

I drew a deep breath and recounted what had happened.

When I was done, Lisa lowered her head. "I should have been there. I'm sorry."

"If you had come," I said, "your parents would have noticed, and when the police came to your house, your parents would have known what you'd been up to. We wouldn't have been able to deny anything. You did the right thing."

"You thought the homeless guy was shot," Colin said. "But I thought *you'd* been shot. So when that lady cop was here, I asked her if anyone had been hurt."

"You did?" I grabbed his arm. "What did she say?"

"She said no." I heaved a tremendous sigh of relief. Colin pulled his arm out of my grasp. "Do you think they'll find your bike?"

"I hope not," I said. A smile flitted across my face. "Then we did it? We actually stopped three people from getting killed?"

Colin and Lisa both smiled and nodded.

"I guess we did," Colin said. He slapped my back and started laughing. "We foiled a heist. That makes us real live crime fighters." He yanked his phone out of his pocket and handed it to me. "Let's call Archer."

I left a message for Archer to meet us at the park, but since the calls the previous night hadn't been returned, I wasn't holding out much hope that he'd be there when we showed up. We walked to the park, laughing and joking, happier than any of us had been in a long time. Even Lisa seemed in good spirits, and I realized it had been a while since I'd seen her really happy.

We'd done what we were supposed to do, and now at least two people who were supposed to die, three if I counted the homeless guy, were alive.

To my surprise, Archer was sitting on a bench, reading a newspaper. We walked across the grass and sat down next to him.

"No ice cream truck today?" Colin asked, laughing.

"It's my day off." For a moment, his tone was chilly. Then he sighed and forced a grin. It was then that I noticed a bruise on his cheek and scratches on his hands.

"Are you okay?" I asked.

He nodded. "Just part of the job, Dean. Just part of the job. I hope you three are taking the day off too. You must have had a pretty busy night. Tell me what happened."

"Well," I began, "it started when things went really bad at the police station…"

Lisa, Colin, and I took turns telling bits of the story, and Archer didn't interrupt once. When we were finished, Archer smiled.

"Excellent job, guys. Very quick thinking. I couldn't be more impressed."

"I'm really sorry I couldn't get out," Lisa said. "I

wanted to. I really did."

"You three are a team, Lisa. Don't worry if sometimes you can't make it to the game. There will be times when you'll need to carry more weight. There is nothing to feel guilty about." He turned to me. "And your parents? How did they take the visit from the police?"

"My mom just cries a lot," I said. "And my dad is really hard to read. I think I'll be having more therapy sessions, even though this coming Friday was supposed to be my last one."

Archer nodded thoughtfully. "Therapy is a small price to pay for three lives, Dean. Remember that. If it means you have to talk about your feelings for a while, it's not a bad thing." He looked each of us square in the face and added, "There are highs and lows with this job, guys. If you feel like you need to talk to a therapist about things, you should feel free to do so."

"But that would compromise the Society, wouldn't it?" Colin said.

"I'd avoid talk about visions and secret societies. But you've all been through a lot. Talk about how you feel about what you've experienced. And talk to each other too."

We nodded, and Archer stood up. "I'll be in touch. In the meantime, get some rest. Be kids for a while." He trained his eyes on me. "I might be out of the city for a few days, but make sure you call if you have any more visions."

"I will."

He grinned. "Great job, you three. Really great job." Then he turned and strode away.

CHAPTER 26

We stopped by the museum several times over the next few days. It was actually hard to stay away from the place. News of the vandalism hit papers on Monday, and pretty much every day thereafter the lineup for admission stretched farther and farther around the side of the building. Sok was nowhere to be found, not near the museum or in the little park across the street. I wasn't entirely sure what I'd say to him if we did see him. He was probably lying low, expecting me to tell the police that I'd seen him. Lisa tried to talk to Sok's grandfather in French a couple of times, but all he said was that Sok was working on convincing people to give the relic back. I thought that was a lot of pressure to put on a fifteen- or sixteen-year-old.

"What do you suppose that means?" Lisa asked.

I shrugged. "I feel bad for the guy, but as long as I'm not having visions, he can do whatever he wants."

Colin nodded. "I agree."

"Even if he's going to try to steal it again?" she asked

"Can you blame him?" Colin asked. "It was stolen from his village first. It's not really stealing if you're just taking something back that belongs to you."

I felt the same way.

Sok wasn't the only one we couldn't find. We also walked all over town searching for the homeless guy who had adopted my bike, but he seemed to have disappeared. I guess almost getting shot would be a pretty strong motivator to move along. My parents hadn't noticed my bike missing yet. They were too busy hammering me with questions every time they got me alone—especially my mom. It seemed she thought I'd grown accustomed to all the attention I'd received over the past couple months and wanted more of it. She kept encouraging me to have my friends from therapy over to hang out. I was getting more attention than a pop star, and none of it was any good. My dad wasn't much better, but he did keep his questions simple.

"Anything you want to tell me, son?" he would ask almost every time we were alone. I figured he knew something was up, I just hoped he didn't know I was the kid who smashed the window at the museum.

Needless to say, I tried to spend as little time as possible at home. We tried to meet up with Archer again too, but he must've still been out of town because he never returned our calls.

When Friday finally arrived, I relaxed. Despite everything my parents had been on me about during the past week, not once had they said I'd have to keep going to therapy after this last session. Hope surged in my chest that this was the last day I'd have to talk about my feelings, the last day I'd have to see Eric or listen to his whiny voice. I waited in my room until it was time to go, not wanting to risk doing something that would make my parents reconsider, and I only came downstairs when my dad called up that it was time to go.

Colin met me on the curb after my dad dropped me off. "Did you get my emails?" he asked when we'd pushed through the main doors.

"No," I said. "I was trying not to make any noise in my room. Why? What was the message?"

Before Colin could speak, I was shoved from behind into the wall. I spun around to face whoever it was, but lost most of my nerve when I saw the giant goon leering over me. "Hi, Rodney." His bottom lip jutted out, and his right eye, bloodshot and deep brown, twitched.

Eric stepped from behind his friend and sneered. "I'm looking forward to tonight, Curse," he said. He gestured to Rodney. "We both are."

I smiled. "Oh, are you two going out on a date? I always thought you made a nice couple."

Colin and a couple of the kids around us laughed.

Eric's cheeks reddened. "You know, Curse, we spend a lot of time in The Field. I can't wait to get you alone in there."

"Huh?" I turned to Colin, and he grimaced. "The Field? What the heck is he talking about?"

"I tried to email you. I only just found out this morning. I guess your mom didn't want you to find out until today."

"Hi, Dean," Rylee said from over my shoulder. "Thanks for the invitation to your party. I've never gone paintballing before. It should be fun." She turned and walked over to the circle of chairs.

Eric growled and got right in my face. "You're so dead." He glanced at Rylee and then back at me and growled again before backing off. A couple of the other kids in the group walked by and thanked me for the invitation. I had no idea what was going on.

"Party?" I looked at Colin as Lisa jogged in.

"Did you tell him?" Lisa asked. She turned to Eric and Rodney. "What do you two jerks want?"

A wicked smile spread across Eric's face. "Oh, I forgot you'll be there too." He rubbed his hands together and glared at each of us in turn. "Payback times three." Rodney laughed deeply, and the two of them stomped away happily.

I turned to my friends. "What the heck is everyone talking about?"

"Your mom," Lisa said. "She's put together some kind of end-of-therapy celebration. She invited everyone to play indoor paintball tonight. I didn't find out until this morning."

"Laser paintball," Colin said with a grin. "It's just like regular paintball only with special effects, like lasers and flashing lights and stuff like that. It actually sounds like a blast." He nodded to Eric and Rodney. "Except they're gonna be there."

"Why didn't she tell me she invited them? Why didn't she tell me about the party at all?"

Lisa smiled. "I heard my parents talking about it last night. Apparently she wants to show you there are safer ways to get attention than acting out, and she thought you'd put up a fuss if you knew about it."

"Safer ways?" Colin laughed. "Clearly your mom has never been shot by a paintball."

"And she invited Eric and Rodney?" I asked again, unwilling to believe she'd do that. "She has to know I hate those guys. I mean, she's heard us talking about them enough."

"She invited everyone," Colin said.

"The place is called World of Paintball," Lisa said quizzically, "so why are they calling it The Field?"

"It's a nickname," Colin said.

"The nickname is The Field?" Lisa laughed. "Not exactly catchy."

"It's not called The Field," Colin said. "That's just what some people say. The real nickname is something else." He paused for effect. "The Killing Field."

CHAPTER 27

Just like Colin said, the place was called World of Paintball, which sounded a bit like an amusement park. But when we pulled into the parking lot, it looked like something else entirely, and I saw why they called it The Killing Field. Cinder block walls painted a drab gray formed sharp right angles that went up about three stories to a flat roof. Spotlights lanced out from the rooftop and rolled across the parking lot. The word "prison" sprang to mind. Rodney was going to feel right at home here.

"All right, kids," my mom said, "I've already taken care of everything with the manager. Just go right in and have fun. Remember to play nice. I'll see you at eleven."

"Play nice?" Colin asked, then leaned toward me and whispered, "Your mom does know we're going to be shooting each other, doesn't she?"

"Thanks, Mrs. Curse," Lisa said happily. "We'll see you at eleven."

"Yeah," I mumbled, "thanks, Mom."

A couple other kids from therapy waved as their parents drove away.

I shivered. The only thing that made this place look like it might be okay were the glass doors leading to the lobby. *Prisons probably don't have glass doors*, I told myself. *Or lobbies for that matter.*

Eric and Rodney shoved past, carrying duffel bags. They seemed far too comfortable in this place, and I wondered how often they came here. The girl behind the counter wore a tight black shirt and a green army-style hat. She had a tattoo on her forearm of something I couldn't make out. She greeted Eric and Rodney with smiles. Yep, it was pretty clear they came here often.

"Listen up," the girl said. She pointed to a long table at the side of the room. "You'll find coveralls, goggles, and masks on the tables over there. Put your gear on and proceed to the next checkpoint through the door."

"Not bad," Colin said, looking down at his paintball suit. "I look like an Army Ranger." He eyed Lisa maliciously. "Better watch your back, girlie."

She laughed and then sighed and jabbed him in the stomach. "Call me girlie again. I dare you."

"Through the doors!" the girl behind the counter shouted. The door led to a platform that overlooked a huge warehouse with corrugated steel walls and a concrete floor. Small barriers had been erected randomly throughout the area, and crossover steps and metal gangways rose all around, offering a height advantage to anyone who managed to claim one as a perch during the game. At first it reminded me of one of those mazes that scientists created for lab mice, but when I looked closer, it was clear it wasn't a maze at all. It would be easy to run straight from one end to the other... except, of course, for the people who might be hiding around the corners waiting to blast you with paintballs.

A voice boomed from somewhere below. "Walk down the stairs to the weapons station."

At the base of the stairs was a long table filled with paintball guns and large metal canisters of compressed air. Two men stood behind the table, their lips pressed into identical lines. The first man was a giant with thick arms and no neck, just a giant head on giant shoulders. He reminded me of one of those WWE wrestlers you see on TV. His head was shaved bald, but he had dark grease streaks all over his face and head, which made him look extra dangerous. The other man was scrawny, with a narrow face and a long, dark goatee that hung from his chin and covered most of his neck.

"We're the judges," the scrawny man said, stroking his goatee. His large partner stood unmoving, hands clasped behind his back, his narrowed eyes moving down the line, sizing us up with a piercing glare. "My name is Dyson," the man with the goatee continued, "and this is Tank." He paused and seemed to dare us to laugh. When no one did, he continued. "We'll show you how to use your weapons, break you into two teams, and then you'll be set loose."

A couple of the girls on my right giggled, and Colin kept rocking back and forth on the balls of his feet like he was preparing to take flight. Pretty much everyone was smiling and I was just starting to think that maybe this wasn't such a bad idea when my gaze fell on Eric and Rodney. They weren't smiling, but they seemed pleased. Their eyes were glued to me in a murderous stare, and they kept rubbing their hands. *Great.*

As if reading my mind, Lisa leaned over and said, "We have guns too, Dean. Being big won't mean a thing out there. In fact, it will just make them easier to hit."

"Good point," I said, feeling a little better.

"First rule," Tank said in a deep voice. "When you're not in the game, you keep your gun pointed down." He plucked a gun from the table and demonstrated.

"The guns can go off by accident," Dyson added, "and if you swing it around, it might go off." Tank raised the gun and swung it wildly at our group. Girls and guys screamed alike, and Rylee, who was standing behind me, grabbed my shoulder.

"Sorry," she whispered, then laughed.

I laughed weakly and managed to say, "Any time." I caught Colin raising his eyebrows at me. He gave an approving and somewhat mischievous nod. I started to turn back to Tank and Dyson and spotted Eric once more. He looked like someone had just shoved a gym sock in his mouth. He kept glancing from me to Rylee.

"Rule two," Dyson said, "if you get shot, shout *Hit!*, raise your gun over your head, and walk back to your team's end zone. And if you're doing the shooting and someone yells *hit*, stop shooting them." A metal man-shaped target popped up on the right, and Tank turned and fired. A paintball splattered across the target's head and then it fell back, but Tank fired again and moved forward until he was standing above the target and then fired at least a dozen more times.

"That," Dyson said when Tank had finished, "is what we *don't* want to see." The metal target rose again, paint dripping down its featureless face.

Eric caught my attention and pointed, first at me and then at the target. Rodney nodded and flashed a creepy, toothy grin that sent a shiver up my back.

"Now," Dyson said, "does anyone have their own guns? We'll need to check them out."

"We do." Eric gave a quick wave.

"No worries, Feldman. We know your guns." He turned to the group. "Anyone else?"

"They brought their own guns?" I whispered.

Rylee spoke from behind me. "I heard that Eric and Rodney play paintball a few times a week."

"Are you kidding me?" Colin asked.

She shook her head. "No, I'm not. I even heard that one of those guys is Rodney's brother."

Colin and I gasped at the same time.

"Rodney has a brother?" Lisa asked.

If it was anyone, it was Tank. The two of them clearly came from the same genetic pool. If he was anything like Rodney, I wasn't sure we'd get out of this alive. Dyson called us forward and handed us our guns. He made each of us take a couple practice shots at the pop-up target, and in a matter of minutes, we were all geared up. I glanced over at Rodney and Eric and suddenly felt very faint. Where our guns were short and boxy, their guns were sleek and professional looking.

Rodney looked like a character out of a war movie. He had a long-barreled gun with a scope resting on his shoulder and a pistol strapped to his thigh. Eric had a smaller weapon, but it was no less menacing than Rodney's.

"Those do shoot paintballs, right?" someone on my right asked, looking at the two bullies.

Colin followed my gaze and said, "Oh wow!" He seemed to forget himself and stepped up to Eric to examine the guns. "That's an MP5, isn't it? And that..." He pointed to the gun strapped to Eric's thigh. "That's a 9 mm, right?" He turned to Rodney. "And that's a Tippman X7 sniper rifle, isn't it?" Colin knew guns not because he had any actual experience with them, but because of video games. He loved his war games and studied the weapons manuals for those games more than he studied history for school.

As an answer, Eric swung around and fired two shots at the metal target and then pulled the pistol from his thigh and fired again. All three shots splattered against the target. "Don't worry, Colin," he said, "you'll be getting a good look at these weapons soon enough."

"Save it for the field," Dyson said.

Eric nodded and turned back to me and tapped the top of his gun, a gesture I took as some kind of warning. If he was trying to freak me out, it was working.

Dyson and Tank divided us right down the middle, forming two teams, and then stepped forward. "Team A," Dyson said, pointing to his right. "Tank will take you to the other side of the warehouse, where you'll find your flag. You'll have just a couple minutes to work out a strategy, and then the game will start."

"Is there a whistle or something?" asked Gavin Richardson, an eleventh grader from the newly formed Team A.

"No whistles," Dyson said, "but don't worry. You'll

know when the game is starting." There was some more giggling as Tank led Team A out of sight and then Dyson turned to us. "Team B, better make your plan."

Rylee waved everyone over, and we all huddled up. "Okay," she said, smiling, "who's played this before?" Colin's hand shot up.

"You've never played this before," I said.

"I did," he said, "Once. But I play Comrade Killer online all the time. It's just like this. Trust me, I know strategy."

"Comrade Killer?" one of the other girls asked.

"It's a war game," Colin said. His smile widened. "If it doesn't work, someone else can lead on the next one."

"Thirty seconds," Dyson shouted for the benefit of the whole warehouse.

"Okay, Colin," Rylee said. "Tell us what to do."

Colin laid out a plan in seconds. My job was to get to one of the gangways on the right and pick off the other team as they ran by. Easy enough if I could get there, but I figured the other team would be thinking the same thing, so I'd have to be fast.

"Five, four, three," Dyson yelled, "two, one." An evil smile spread across Dyson's face. "Welcome to... *The Killing Field!*"

CHAPTER 28

The atmosphere in the room changed instantly. The large overhead lights flicked out and were replaced by black lights that illuminated all kinds of graffiti around the building that had, up until then, been invisible. Strobe lights flashed, and thin beams of red, green, blue, and yellow lights lanced out from the ceiling and surrounding walls. In a flash, everyone except the two people Colin had designated to stay behind to guard the flag surged forward.

I hunched and sprinted for the gangway. There were at least a few seconds when I wouldn't have to worry about getting shot. The gangway was closer to our base so I didn't have far to go. I spun around corners without looking and made it to the metal staircase in a flash. I climbed the steps and positioned myself behind a piece of plywood that leaned loosely against the metal railing. I squinted through the plastic face mask and strained to see movement. The flashing lights made the whole building look alive. My pulse raced with anticipation. I hadn't even pulled the trigger yet, and I already loved this game.

The sound of rapid fire filled the air like a muffled

burst of firecrackers.

"Hit!" I heard it shouted more than once, along with excited screams and voices shouting directions to one another. The voices were raised to be heard above the ambient ruckus of explosions and futuristic laser blasts. Then something moved on the floor below, just to the right of one of the walls. I took aim and squeezed the trigger. No one yelled "Hit!" and more movement flitted around the floor below. I shot as fast as I could squeeze the trigger, not really aiming, just raining down paintballs as fast and furiously as I could. When I stopped to reload, the sniveling, mocking voice of Eric Feldman rose up from below.

"Missed me, Curse."

I had just refilled my ammo when something the size of my fist landed beside me. I picked it up and squeezed it. It was like a squishy mass of plastic that seemed to be getting harder and harder in my hand. Sweat rolled into my eyes, and it took a couple blinks before I recognized the shape of the object as a plastic grenade.

Toys? I thought. *They're throwing toys at me so that I... what? Run away thinking it's a real grenade?* I squeezed the grenade again; it was rock hard now. I held it up, thinking I might as well send it back over the edge, but just as I was about to toss it over, it exploded... Well, it didn't so much as explode as it *popped*. Like a water balloon, only somehow pressurized. In a blink, I was covered in yellow paint. I used the back of my hand to wipe the plastic face shield and looked around. I immediately recognized Eric and Rodney climbing up from either end of the gangway.

"Paint grenade," Eric said triumphantly. He looked at Rodney. "Did you hear him yell 'hit'?"

Rodney shook his head. "Maybe he's not hit yet."

In the two or three seconds it took for me to realize what was happening and to formulate the thought to yell "Hit!" Eric and Rodney must've unloaded fifty paintballs at me. It felt like something between a hornet's sting and being stuck naked in a hail storm. When the word finally came out of my mouth in a shriek of desperation, the two jerks turned and ran away, laughing.

I limped back down the metal staircase and back to our end zone, where my team was celebrating with laughter and high fives.

"You got their flag?" I croaked.

They turned, and all excitement drained from their faces.

"Dean?" Lisa asked. "Is that you?"

"What happened?" Colin said.

"Rodney and Eric," I said.

"Did they bring paint brushes or something?" Colin started laughing, as did everyone else. I was in far too much pain to laugh at myself.

Dyson walked up and nodded knowingly. "Looks like

the third-generation GPM-12 paint grenade. Those are single-use and pretty expensive." He looked me up and down. "Pretty effective."

"Did they shoot you too?" Colin asked.

I shrugged. "Um, yeah. I think I was hit a couple times." I turned back to the team. "At least we got their flag."

"Oh, we got it all right," Rylee said as more high fives were exchanged. "Colin's strategy worked perfectly." Colin bowed.

"Good," I said. "If I'm going to get painted up like this, we better at least win."

"Round two begins in thirty seconds," Dyson said.

I rolled my shoulders and tried to block out the stinging pain. "Round two. Good. Time for some payback."

Colin called the play again. This time he let me stay back and guard the flag with Rylee. All we had to do was hunker down behind a wooden crate and pick off anyone who got close to the flag.

"Thanks again for inviting me, Dean," Rylee said as she hunkered down beside me once the game was underway. "I'm glad I came. I meant to ask if you were okay. Last time I saw you, museum security was dragging you away."

"Yeah," I said without hesitating. "I'm fine. It's all sorted out."

"Good." No sooner had the words left her mouth than

a yellow splatter of paint covered her face mask. "Hit!" she yelled. I flattened behind the crate while she stood up, lifted her gun over her head, and walked over to the safe zone.

I lifted my gun and fired off a couple shots in the direction the blasts had come from. Then a yellow blast hit the ammo container on my gun and knocked it off. I managed two more shots until I started shooting blanks. My paint balls had scattered all over the ground, and I was about to reach for one when Eric stepped into our end zone, his MP5 leveled at his shoulder. He fired a couple shots that struck a few inches in front of my feet and then laughed.

"You again?" he said. "We were hoping for Colin or Lisa this time."

We, I thought. *Where's Rodney?* My question was answered a second later when my coveralls were pulled from behind and something round and rubbery was shoved down my back, against my bare skin.

CHAPTER 29

To be fair, when the grenade popped, it really didn't hurt. It just felt like a water balloon popping. Still, I yelled "Hit!" right away so I couldn't be shot, and I stood uncomfortably as paint oozed down my back, into my pants, and down my legs. It was disgusting, and I wondered if any of my clothes were salvageable.

There were three more rounds after that, and in the end Eric and Rodney's team won three, while we only won twice. By the time we finished, Colin had gotten peppered with so many paintballs that he was as yellow as I was, although I was probably more yellow underneath the coveralls. Eric and Rodney were like a pair of super soldiers, picking off anyone and everyone.

"Guns down," Dyson barked. Everyone did as they were told and pointed the barrels of their weapons to the floor. "Good battle," he said. "We get a lot of people who want to pretend to be commandos for a day, and none of them have been as good as you guys."

I was pretty sure it was something he said to everyone who came for a round of paintball, or at least every group of kids, but I pretended it wasn't. Even though we had only won twice, Colin beamed, and I couldn't help but smile too. For someone who had only played once before, he did amazingly well as a leader. I almost laughed. He wasn't going to let me—or anyone else, for that matter—forget his hand in the victories. Who would have thought that he'd be able to translate all those hours of online game play into real life?

Eric and Rodney looked smugly at me from a couple feet away. I wanted revenge for what they'd done out there, but I wasn't a match for them. They had experience, but more importantly, they had all the toys. Eric's family was so rich that we'd never have a fair fight.

I looked back toward Colin and was about to congratulate him again when the red and yellow blotches of paint on everyone's coveralls suddenly turned gray. I blinked. I wondered if it was a trick of the light, or something to do with everyone being dressed in camouflage. I even thought that maybe I'd taken a blast in the eyes from those darn lasers.

So when Sok suddenly stepped up out of nowhere, wearing some kind of dark turtleneck and black pants, and looked at me with hollow eyes, I wondered when he had joined the game and how my mom had managed to track him down to invite him in the first place. Then his head tilted and his eyes and mouth widened. But I was ready. I recognized what was happening and braced myself for the scream. And it came with a vengeance. Only it wasn't from Sok; it was from my right. I spun around and found myself face to face with the twisted expressions of not one, but two of the security guards from the museum. Instinctively, I brought my arms up to shield myself, and my finger clenched around the trigger of the gun. There were two quick bursts, then some screams, then the vision of Sok shrieked and I jumped again, sending a new burst of paintballs into the crowd.

"Gun down, gun down!" Dyson screamed.

I took a couple slow breaths to compose myself as I started to see colors again, and then I turned to the group. "I'm sorry," I said, lowering the barrel. "It was an accident. I thought I... um... I just got scared," I finally said. I hung the gun at my side and took in the carnage. My carnage. To my surprise, it wasn't as bad as I thought it'd be. Most of the people must've hit the deck right away, and after a couple seconds almost everyone started to laugh.

There were, however, a few people who bore fresh spatters of red paint. Rylee was rubbing a red spot on her thigh.

"I'm sorry," I said.

She shrugged, then smiled and shook her head.

"You're gonna pay for that," Eric's sniveling voice said from a few feet away. I turned, hoping that he'd have a nice red burst right between his eyes, but he didn't seem to be in pain at all. He had a bunch of paint splatters on his coveralls, but those were from the actual game. Rodney, on the other hand, was on the ground, sniffling and clutching the side of his face. Red paint oozed through his fingers.

"Oh, man, Rodney," I said, "I'm sorry about that."

"Relax," Dyson said, "it happens at least once a day." He looked around the room. "It's just paint, people. Unless you've been shot in the eye or something, just shake it off. It's not like Dean did it on purpose. Sometimes the adrenaline from the game makes you kind of twitchy. Let's just keep your finger off the trigger, okay?"

I nodded, and then felt suddenly ill. The weight of what had just happened settled on me. Two guards were going to die... and this time I was sure Sok was also going to die. Why did that kid have to keep putting himself in danger? I glanced at my watch: 10:47 p.m. "What are you planning, Sok?" I muttered. "Why can't you just leave it alone?"

"Now he's talking to himself," Eric said.

I gave my head a shake and glared at Eric. I wished I'd had enough sense to point the gun at him when the vision had startled me.

"Just you wait, Curse," Eric continued. "You have no idea what we're going to do to you, but it's going to—" Two quick bursts of compressed gas erupted from the crowd, and Eric's eyes widened as a gasp escaped his suddenly gaping mouth. A fresh splash of red paint stained his chest, and there was a yellow spatter of paint on his crotch. He dropped to his knees and then fell over whimpering. Lisa smiled and handed a gun she must've borrowed back to the girl beside her. At the same time, Colin turned around and ducked to the back of the group. Everyone was laughing, and I was just impressed that both of them had had the same thought at the same time.

"And that's the end of the game, kids," Dyson said quickly. "Turn in your guns to Tank and put your coveralls on the table by the stairs, then out you go." He gestured to the illuminated exit sign at the top of the metal staircase. "Come again."

CHAPTER 30

My mom was waiting in the lobby when we got there, and after a brief, startled glance at my painted clothing, she was all smiles. She'd done this for me, and I knew she had meant well. I forced a grin, which really wasn't easy considering I was in physical pain, covered in paint, and trying desperately to work out exactly how we were going to save Sok and the security guards... AGAIN.

Everyone thanked my mom and me for the fun evening. Eric and Rodney wandered into the lobby after everyone else was gone. Eric was limping, and Rodney was still holding his neck, but the two of them put on their most innocent faces and thanked my mom too, adding that they couldn't wait for the next time I could hang out with them. I resisted the urge to slug Eric, relying instead on the memory of him getting shot in the groin to brighten my mood. My mom beamed.

"Ten forty-seven," I muttered to Lisa and Colin while we walked to the parking lot. "Sok and two guards."

Colin cursed under his breath. "What is that stupid monk doing?"

"I told you we should have tried harder to find him," Lisa said.

We rode the rest of the way answering questions from my mom and raving about how much fun it was. Colin took the lead and told how he'd managed to guide the team to two victories. He left out the part about how that had only happened because Eric and Rodney were trying harder to attack us than they were trying to win.

The next morning I woke up to an email from Lisa telling me to come over. After breakfast, and some teasing from Becky for still having a few spots of yellow paint on my skin, I said good-bye to my parents and ran to Lisa's place.

Lisa's house was small, one-story, and green, which was funny because her last name was Green. Both her parents did shift work, and usually we didn't hang out at her place because one of them was always sleeping. On that particular Saturday, Lisa was home alone, and Colin was already there.

"You really need to get a new cell phone," Colin said. "We've been waiting an hour for you to get over here."

I checked my watch. "It's eight o'clock in the morning. You've been here since seven? Since when do you ever get up before noon on a weekend?"

"I would have come at six if I thought Lisa was awake. We have to figure out what we're doing about this," Colin said. "We've already left a message for Archer to meet us in the park at nine o'clock, or as soon as he can, but if he's still not around, we don't really have a lot of options." He was trying to keep his voice steady, but I could hear the panic.

Lisa shook her head. "I already told him we just need to go to the museum again. It'll be better this time. We'll call the police sooner."

"And I told her," Colin said angrily, "that it barely worked last time, and we almost didn't make it out of there. Something she would have known if she had been there."

Lisa's face flushed, and she opened her mouth to speak, only to clamp it shut again.

"Look, guys, there's no point in fighting. Lisa did the right thing by not coming that night, and Colin, you know it. We all could have been in a lot more trouble if she'd snuck out and gotten caught." Colin looked down at his shoes, and I hesitated just long enough for a breath before I spoke again. "You already called Archer, so let's just go to the park and see if he's there."

"And if he's not?" Lisa asked.

"If he's not, then we'll think of a plan on our own. But I think he'll be there. In fact, I'm sure he'll be there. C'mon, let's go."

Nine o'clock came and went, and Archer didn't show. At eleven o'clock, we called Archer again and left another message. By noon, we'd come to the conclusion that he wasn't in town and we were on our own.

"He should've given you a number for the others in the Society," Colin said. "How can he expect us to rely on just him when he's running around saving the people in his own visions?"

Lisa sighed and looked at me. "So what do you think we should do?"

"I've been thinking about that a lot," I said. "We tried to stop Sok last time, and all it did was delay him. If we manage to stop him again, there's no guarantee he won't try again in the next museum."

"And?" Colin asked.

"And what if it's in Budapest or something, and I get a vision that he's got twenty-four hours to live? There's not a whole lot I'll be able to do to stop it, that's what."

Colin nodded. "Then what? You think we should actually turn him in? Get him arrested?"

"We can't do that, Dean," Lisa said firmly. "He's not a typical thief. He's just trying to get something back that rightfully belongs to his ancestral village. He's not a criminal."

Colin rolled his eyes. "Better he's locked up than dead. Wouldn't you say?"

"Stop it!" I said. "Just stop." Their eyes widened at the sternness of my tone. "We need to work together on this. Besides, I have a plan."

"To turn them in?" Colin asked.

"No," I answered. "I think you're right. He doesn't deserve jail time."

"But you were right too," Lisa said. "He might try again somewhere you can't intervene. Then he'll be dead. And Colin has a point that being locked up is a lot better than being dead. I mean, he doesn't deserve to go to jail, but it's a better option than death." Colin grinned and gave Lisa a thankful nod. *At least they're not fighting anymore*, I thought.

"I know," I said. "That's why we can't let that happen either."

"Then what?" Colin asked. "I don't see any other option here."

"There's one," I said, hesitantly.

"Well?" Lisa asked. "Spill already. What's the other option?"

I drew a deep breath and let it out slowly. "We steal it," I said. "We steal the relic."

CHAPTER 31

"You're crazy." Lisa paced in a tight circle around the bench Colin and I were sitting on.

"I agree," Colin said. "I mean, it's one thing to stop a robbery; it's another thing altogether to actually be the robbers."

"Keep your voices down," I said, glancing at the people strolling by. Lisa sighed and sat back on the bench with us, and I lowered my voice to a whisper. "It's not ideal, I know that. But we're talking about a life here. Three of them, actually."

"What if we die?" Lisa said.

"We won't," I answered. "If we were going to die, I'd have had a vision of it. Archer shook each of our hands, so he'd be here too, telling us we were going to die."

"We can still be arrested," Colin said after a brief pause.

"Like you said, better arrested than dead."

"I was talking about Sok. Not us!" He shook his head. "I'm too pretty for prison."

"Don't flatter yourself," Lisa said.

"Guys," I said, "we don't have a lot of time, so how about this: let's just think of a way to get the relic. Hypothetically speaking, how would we do it? If we can't think of a good plan, we go to plan B and, I dunno, get some duct tape and tape Sok and his French conspirators to a tree in the park or something."

"I like that idea," Colin said. "I'll even pay for the duct tape."

"Hypothetically," Lisa began, "you'd probably have to go in through the roof the way you saw Sok's little gang going in."

"We don't have a van," I said. "And we'd be spotted carrying a huge ladder down the street. We'd never get up there."

"We could use a grappling hook," Colin said.

"Colin, you can't even climb the rope in gym glass," Lisa said. "How the heck do you think you're going to climb a rope up the side of a building?" She hesitated and then added, "Do you even know where to buy a grappling hook?"

"I could find one," Colin muttered.

"Lisa's right," I said. "Besides, we'd probably get lost or stuck in the ventilation shafts and die of starvation or something."

"And," Lisa added, "hypothetically, we can't break a window to get in since you did that and the alarms started up right away, right? We'd never have time to get in and get out without the guards getting us."

I nodded. "Okay, so no getting in through the roof and no getting in through breaking glass. What's left?"

"Nothing," Lisa said. "There's nothing left."

Colin tapped his chin thoughtfully. "Well, there is something."

"There's another way?" I asked.

He nodded.

"A way that doesn't have anything to do with a movie you saw?" Lisa asked, huffing.

He nodded again.

"Are you going to share it with the rest of us?" I asked.

He smiled slyly. "Do you guys remember when I stood in that caveman exhibit?"

I nodded, and Lisa said, "I know you fit in with them, Colin. But I think they'd notice a real live boy standing in the display. Pretending to be mannequins will not work."

His smile spread. "Don't you remember the door?"

I did. The door Colin fell through. The door behind the caveman display. "It was unlocked," I muttered under my breath.

"It was unlocked," Colin repeated. "It's a huge storage area filled with crates, boxes, and display boards. Tons of places to hide. We could sneak in, hide until the right time, and then, *presto*, steal the head and make a run for it." He checked his watch. "Museum closes at five o'clock today. We only have a few hours."

"Whoa," Lisa said. "Just hang on a second. Now you're on board with Dean's plan?" Colin shrugged. "This was supposed to be hypothetical," Lisa continued. "And remember, hypothetically speaking, you get caught stealing from a museum, you go to jail or juvenile detention or somewhere like that. You think Rodney and Eric are bullies? I bet those places are filled with people that even Rodney would be scared of."

I shivered at that thought. But given the options, and the fact that we were up against the clock, I didn't see much of a choice. I started muttering to myself. "We could call the police on Sok, but that would only delay the inevitable. If I got another vision of him a week or a month from now, and he was too far away for me to do anything, then I'd be responsible for his death." I shook my head. "I can't be responsible for that. I'd say we could try to find him and talk him out of it, but even if we found him, it probably wouldn't do any good. He'd never believe us. The best we could do is threaten to call the cops, but then he'd just try again later, and we'd just be back where we started."

"Talking to yourself is a sign of mental instability," Colin said. "I might need to mention this little one-sided conversation to Dr. Mickelsen."

"Can you not make jokes right now?" Lisa said coldly.

"We're discussing committing a crime here."

Colin rolled his eyes but kept his mouth clamped shut. Several minutes of silence followed while I considered our options. Lisa looked strained, and I was pretty sure she was struggling to find an alternative too. Everything came back to the fact that the only real way to resolve this was to get the relic back to Sok. And since he and his village had already tried every legal way to do that, the only options that remained were the illegal ones.

"I don't see that we have any choice," I said finally.

"What about just going back to Detective Peters?" Lisa said.

"I thought you were against that," I said.

She bit her lip. "I was, but..."

"What would we say?" I asked. "That Sok is going to break in? What will that accomplish? At the very best a delay." I shook my head. "He'd just try again later."

"Maybe," Lisa said. "Or maybe he wouldn't."

"That's the point, Lisa," Colin said. "How can we risk it? If Dean has a vision three months from now, what are we supposed to do?"

"I know all that," Lisa snapped. "I just think there's a way to do this without going to jail."

"Yeah, there is. Don't get caught," Colin said. "If you have a better idea, let's hear it."

Lisa paced around the park bench for several

minutes. Every so often she'd make a move to speak, only to shake her head and continue on. Finally, she plopped back on the bench and sighed. "Fine. Let's do it. But we better not get caught."

CHAPTER 32

We ran home to get dark clothes to change into at the museum and to arrange things with our parents. The plan was the easy part; we had that sorted out before we got back to our block. Sok and the guards were supposed to die at 10:47, so we'd steal the relic before 10:00. We'd just go through any door we could on the way out and sprint for cover. The alarm would go off, but we didn't have an alternative, and Colin was sure we could make it.

We told our parents we were going to hang out at the mall for a few hours and then catch a double-feature at the theater. My dad said he'd pick us up outside the theater at 11:00, but my mom insisted that I clean my room before going out—a feat that took nearly two hours. When I finished, she kissed my head and told me to have a good time. I just about laughed.

I met Lisa and Colin at the bus stop. Colin had his bag stuffed with goodies again, but this time I was grateful. We needed to be prepared for contingencies, and Colin's mind was filled with every heist movie ever made. He probably had thought through a lot more scenarios than I had.

It was 3:30 when we stepped off the bus at the museum, and you'd have thought the entire town had come out that day. The crowd of protestors was surprisingly mellow, which I assumed had something to do with being blamed for the broken window and the increased number of police on the scene. Sok wasn't anywhere near the entrance, and he didn't seem to be in the crowd, either. *Probably getting ready for his theft*, I thought.

There must've been a hundred people just inside the main entrance. It sounded like there were hundreds more throughout the corridors; their voices mashed into a mix of gibberish that sounded like angry birds. A woman bumped into my shoulder, then a moment later, a man knocked into me from behind, grabbed my arm, and apologized before disappearing into the crowd. I panicked, remembering that I had to be careful who I touched and trying to figure out if he'd touched my skin or just my shirt and if that even mattered.

I darted for the wall and plastered myself to it. "I... I didn't get their names," I said.

Lisa and Colin looked around confused. "Who?" Colin asked.

"Did you touch someone?" Lisa said.

Everywhere I looked, I saw potential visions, and for a few brief seconds, I was frozen with fear. I could picture the man and woman perfectly, but I knew I'd never seen them before and had no idea who they were. If I had a vision of either one of them, I'd never find them.

"It was a man and a woman," I said. "They're gone."

"Tell us what they looked like and we'll get their names for you," Lisa said hurriedly.

I stammered through a description, but when I looked around, I saw dozens of people who matched the description, and by the worried expressions on Colin and Lisa's faces, I could see they were thinking the same thing. I was the only one who would be able to recognize them again.

"There are too many people in here, Dean," Colin said. "You're going to be nudged and jostled a hundred times in this place."

"I just need a place to hide out," I said.

"Like a big storage room behind cavemen?" Colin asked.

Lisa shook her head. "It's not going to work. There are too many people. Someone will spot us if we try to sneak into that room. We'll be caught."

"It has to work," I said, not really believing that it was possible myself.

Colin smiled. He cinched the straps on his bag. "Let's just get you to the caveman exhibit and then we'll do what James Bond would do."

Lisa rolled her eyes. "Shoot someone?"

"What? No. Well, he might do that I guess. But that's not what I meant. James Bond would do something else." He lowered his chin and glanced around covertly. "He'd create a diversion."

We moved one foot at a time. As we made our way down the corridor, Colin and Lisa formed a buffer around me, taking the brunt of any physical contact. Even with their bodies shielding me, I was still nudged twice more, and both times the people vanished into the crowd before I could figure out who they were, or even get a good look at them.

"Okay, Mr. Bond," Lisa said when we were positioned in front of the caveman exhibit. "What now?"

Colin dropped his bag from his shoulder and grinned. "Just be ready to run."

"We don't even know if it's still unlocked," I said.

"No time to check," he said. "Not unless you want to risk getting knocked around by a hundred more people."

I shuddered. "No. We need to do this now."

"You're not going to do anything stupid, are you?" Lisa asked, eyeing Colin cautiously. "Nothing that would start a panic in here, right?"

Colin paused for a second and tapped his chin. "Don't

worry, Lisa, I know what I'm doing."

As Colin disappeared into the crowd, Lisa muttered, "Why is it that whenever Colin tells me not to worry, I feel like puking?"

CHAPTER 33

Lisa's comment about wanting to puke couldn't have been more fitting for what Colin had in mind. He was back beside us a couple minutes later, and we didn't even have time to ask him what he'd done before a sharp stench drifted down the corridor. It was like rotting eggs, fermented fish, and moldy cheese all rolled together in an invisible cloud.

Hands shot up as people covered their noses and made for the exit. One woman even rushed to a garbage can and vomited, and I thought I heard others doing the same farther down the corridor. I pulled the collar of my shirt up over my nose, and Lisa gagged. Colin stood beside us coughing.

"L—Lisa, you go first," Colin sputtered. He waited until the corridor was thick with people heading for the exit, everyone moving together, heads down, eyes watering. No one was shoving or looking especially panicked, but they were moving at a steady pace. "Go," he said.

Lisa didn't hesitate. She stepped over the rope and kept hunched. I held my breath as she turned the doorknob and slid through the doorway. From what I could see, no one noticed.

"G—Go, Dean," Colin choked. "Now."

I followed Lisa's example of keeping low and scrambled behind the bushes at the back of the display then through the door. Colin clambered through on my heels. The door closed with a satisfying *click* and Colin set the deadbolt.

The air felt fresh compared to what we'd just left. I blinked away the stinging in my eyes and took a moment to look at where we were. Three metal steps descended from a short platform beside the door. The room was huge, with a concrete floor and cinder block walls painted a dreary gray. Three skylights dotted the ceiling and let in wide beams of sunlight that reflected off the dust in the air. Shelves filled with boxes and artifacts covered most of the perimeter walls, and massive crates, easily big enough to fit three or four kids my size, filled up most of the floor space. At the back, wide metal doors were framed with a thin line of sunlight from outside. It was obviously the loading dock where artifacts and supplies were delivered.

"Did anyone see you guys?" Lisa asked.

"Nope," Colin said.

We'd done it. Well, part of it. I smiled. "Nice move, double-oh-seven. What was that, some kind of stink bomb?"

Colin chuckled. "You won't find these stink bombs in your average gag-shop." He reached into his pocket and pulled out a glass vial about the size of his finger filled with a translucent yellow liquid. "These are Israeli military-grade stink bombs. They use them to stop riots. I got them a couple months ago from a guy online. They cost me a hundred bucks each." I vaguely remembered Colin talking about them a while back, but he bought so many weird things online that I hadn't really given it much thought.

"Why would you buy something like that?" Lisa asked.

Colin looked from Lisa to me and back to Lisa again. "Um, did you hear me say 'military-grade stink bombs'? How could I *not* buy them? I was going to break one in Eric's locker when school started." He pondered for a minute. "But now I think I better save them in case we need them for another mission."

"For once, your weirdness has paid off," Lisa said.

"How many did you use out there?" I asked.

"Just one," he said proudly. "I have a few more, but the smell hit me so hard when I broke the vial that I figured I didn't need any more. Don't worry. If they find it and clean it up, they can air out the building pretty fast." He gestured to the room. "We better find a hiding place before someone comes in here. We still have hours to wait."

We found a place to hide behind a stack of empty crates and a large two-dimensional plywood teepee leaning against the wall. We didn't speak for the better part of an hour. We could hear the odd voice carry through the door, but couldn't tell if the voices were guards or patrons. If we could hear them, we worried that our voices might carry through from our side. At 4:30 p.m., a voice came over the PA system announcing that the museum would be closing in thirty minutes.

"I'm going to explore this place," Colin said.

"Just wait until they're closed," Lisa said sternly. "What if they come in here?"

"They'll be chasing people out for the next thirty minutes," he said. "I'm just going to have a look around."

Lisa looked at me to back her up, but I just shrugged. Colin wouldn't listen to me anyway, and he was probably right. "Try not to make any noise," I said.

Lisa glared and then sighed, defeated. "Just remember what's at stake, Colin."

"Just remember what's at stake, Colin," Colin echoed in a whiney, high-pitched whisper. He stood, pushed himself to his feet, hunched over, and headed out to explore the boxes.

Lisa rubbed her palms on her jeans, and I realized her hands were shaking. She noticed me watching and shoved them under her legs. Her ears reddened almost immediately. I was reminded of how Dr. Mickelsen had neglected to say that Lisa was coping well.

"Are you okay, Lisa?"

The muscles in her jaw flexed. "Of course I am. Why do you ask?"

"I just thought maybe... I mean, if you want to talk about something. Anything..." I sighed. "Lisa, something is obviously wrong, and I really want you to talk to me about it. You've been there for me from the beginning. I owe you."

"You don't." She took a few deep breaths, and I saw a glint of moisture in her eyes. "It's not a big deal, it's just... sometimes I get scared that I'm going to do something to mess this up." She picked at one of the crates nearby. "I'm worried I'll be the reason we fail. It's not like we get a second shot at this stuff. We fail and someone dies. I don't want to be the reason someone dies. Plus, my parents don't think I'm coping with Mrs. Farnsworthy's death very well anyway, and they're making me keep going to therapy at least until school starts."

I nodded. "Maybe it will help. But you don't need to feel bad about how you feel. I mean, jeez, I feel like that every time I have a vision. Sometimes I'm so afraid I can hardly breathe."

"But you get up and try every time," she said.

"So do you."

Her face flushed again, and she chewed her lip. "My parents weren't awake the other night."

I blinked. "What?"

"The night that you and Colin went to the museum, I could've come. My mom was working, and my dad was sound asleep. But I was so afraid that I'd do something to mess it up. It was supposed to be an easy mission and—"

"Lisa," I said, "you don't need to explain. One of these days I'm going to feel like that, and you and Colin are going to have to pick up the slack. We're a team. You don't need to feel guilty." She nodded weakly, and I added, "And I used to think that our failure meant that I had caused someone to die, but that's not the way it is. You heard Archer, right? Someone is going to die, and we have a shot at giving them more time. That's all. We're not going to save everyone. I think I realized that the day Mr. Utlet died. But we've saved people, Lisa." I nudged her leg. "You are one of the reasons my sister is still alive. I couldn't have done that without you and Colin."

She sighed, and a real grin flicked at her lips. "Do you think Colin is having trouble coping with any of this?" We craned our necks around the plywood teepee and saw Colin having a fake conversation with an Egyptian sarcophagus. He glanced back and saw us looking, then promptly wrapped his arms around the artifact in a passionate embrace and pretended to make out with it. We both laughed.

"He's dealing with it the best he knows how," I said, chuckling. "Plus, I'm pretty sure he thinks this is all some hidden camera reality show." I was about to whisper across the room at him when I noticed that he'd stopped moving and his gaze was fixed on the door. Then I heard what he must've heard.

The rattle of a handle and *click* of the door unlocking.

CHAPTER 34

Lisa yanked me back as the door opened. We peeked through the crates and made out the silhouette of a guard standing in the doorway. *Colin*, I thought. I tried to look around the teepee again, but I couldn't spot him, and I didn't dare risk sticking my head out farther.

The guard closed the door behind him and walked down the steps into the bay. He must've flicked the light switch by the door, because the large overhead lights flickered and then turned on. I felt completely exposed. We should've found a better hiding place. I should have backed Lisa up when she told Colin to stay put. I groaned inwardly.

The guard drew a series of deep breaths and let them out slowly. He looked like he was in his early twenties, with dark spiky hair and a dark complexion—not one of the guards from my visions. He sauntered casually across the bay to the loading doors and gave them a good shake. *He's doing his rounds*, I thought. Checking to make sure all the doors are locked. I checked my watch—it was 5:14—and wondered if this was something we'd need to be worried about every hour or just something they did once after closing.

He picked his way between the rows of artifacts and props and came to an abrupt stop when he got to the Egyptian sarcophagus, the same one Colin had been making out with moments before. The guard glanced back at the door and then bent over, disappearing below a shelf of goods. Lisa's hand felt like a vise on my shoulder, and I think we both expected the guard to stand up holding Colin by the ear or something. Instead the guard popped up holding a curved sword and began battling what I could only assume were invisible pirates.

Lisa and I glanced at each other, her unhinged jaw matching my own, and then we turned back and watched the guard maneuver around statues and over boxes. As shocking as it was when the guy started playing with the sword, after a few seconds I had to clamp my hand over my mouth and pinch my leg hard to stop from laughing. Lisa was struggling not to laugh too, and even though the last thing I wanted was for us to get caught, I had to admit that it was good to see her smiling.

The door suddenly flew open with a *clang*, and the spiky-haired guard dropped his sword to the ground.

"What are you doing?" a gruff voice called from the doorway. "It shouldn't take you more than thirty seconds to check the door. And did I just see you waving a sword around?"

"No," the spiky-haired guard answered. "It was, um, just... I mean, I was just, um, picking it up off the floor." He quickly bent and plucked the sword from the floor and placed it on one of the nearby crates. "The loading bay is good. Everything's checked."

The guard at the door groaned. "Hurry up, rookie, there's more building to check."

The guard scampered back up the steps, flicked the light off, and disappeared through the door. Lisa sighed beside me, and a moment later, Colin's head popped up from somewhere near the sarcophagus. He moved quickly back to our hiding place and let out a sigh of relief when he was hidden beside us again.

"Whew, that was close," he said.

"We stay in here from now on," I said. "Lisa was right. It's too important to risk being caught for a little exploring or so that you can make out with your girlfriend's coffin again."

Colin laughed and nodded. "You have to admit, she's quite the hottie."

"Or at least she would have been a couple thousand years ago," Lisa said.

For the next few hours, we passed the time as quietly as possible. Colin talked about how we should challenge Eric and Rodney to a rematch at The Killing Field, an idea I wasn't too keen on until he mentioned that his dad had promised to buy him a couple top-of-the-line guns.

"They shoot over two hundred paintballs a minute," he said. "Those two jerks won't have a chance." He smiled when both Lisa and I said we'd consider it, and then he smiled even wider when Lisa asked what he'd brought in his backpack. He pulled out each item, held it up so we could get a look, and then replaced it:

- Three rolls of duct tape
- Twelve feet of rope
- A block of cheddar cheese
- Six mouse traps
- Four Roman candles
- Lady finger firecrackers
- Water bottle
- Needle and thread
- Roll of tinfoil
- Four Israeli military-grade stink bombs
- BBQ lighter
- Pocket knife
- Glow stick

Lisa and I shook our heads when he was done, both wondering the same thing, no doubt: why in the world did Colin bring so much junk? Colin had reasons for everything, and none of them made much sense. Though, to be fair, the stink bomb did do the trick.

"I would have brought my walkie-talkies," Colin added after showing us everything, "except that *someone* decided to give one to a homeless guy along with his bike." That reminded me that I still needed to get my bike back.

By nine-thirty, we'd slipped into our dark clothes, and by ten, using only the moonlight that filtered through the skylights, we crept to the door, unlocked it, and opened it just a crack. I cursed internally when I saw that same spiky-haired security guard sitting on the edge of the caveman display, humming along to the tune pounding in his earphones. I moved so that Lisa and Colin could see what we were up against, and both of them groaned.

"What do we do?" Colin whispered.

"We wait," Lisa answered.

CHAPTER 35

The minutes ticked by agonizingly slowly, each one bringing us that much closer to when Sok and his gang of thieves were going to get here and, shortly thereafter, die. I was just about to tell Colin to break another one of his stink bombs when heavy footsteps sounded from down the hallway.

"Rookie!" It was the same gruff voice from before. "You're not getting off to a very good start. First I find you sword fighting in the loading bay; now you're slacking off with the cavemen. At this rate, you're going to lose your job before your first paycheck."

"I was just taking my break," the other guard said.

"Your break was over fifteen minutes ago!"

There were more words I couldn't quite make out, along with the sounds of footsteps disappearing down the corridor. We waited another couple minutes for good measure before we peeked out the door again.

It was clear.

We kept low and hid behind the plastic bushes in the caveman exhibit. Beads of sweat formed on my forehead, and I swiped them away with the sleeve of my shirt. "Ready?" I whispered.

Lisa and Colin nodded, and together we stepped into the deserted corridor.

Museums are kind of creepy during the day. I mean, they are filled with dusty old junk, ancient treasures that probably have curses on them, and things that have been dead for a really long time. But they're even worse at night. The bulbs mounted overhead gave off a strange blue light that made the shadows stretch and climb the walls. Some of the mannequins had an evil glow about them that made them look strangely alive and, at times, like they were smiling, as if they knew something we didn't, and found it hilarious. It was like a haunted house, only ten times worse because there were actual dead things hanging around. My heart was hammering like a machine gun blasting away in my chest, and if I listened carefully, I thought I could hear Lisa's and Colin's doing the same.

Just behind us was the medieval weapons exhibit, and I briefly wondered if it would be smart to grab a spear or a mace or some other weapon. Lisa caught me looking and nudged my arm, urging me forward. We crept like the thieves we were about to become and ducked behind the plastic shrubs and ferns beneath the giant T. rex skeleton. I checked my watch: 10:17.

"We're taking too long," I said. "Sok could be here

any second."

Colin nodded and pointed to the metal ball contraption we'd seen the last time we were here. "If we duck behind that, we can make it to the Buddha head from behind. We should go one at a time. I'll go first."

Lisa and I nodded, and Colin hunched and sprinted over to the Rube Goldberg machine and disappeared behind it. I was about to follow him when Lisa grabbed my shoulder and pulled me back into the plastic bushes. Her finger was pressed tightly to her lips, and her eyes were giant disks.

"What?" I mouthed. She pointed toward the Buddha head, and I saw a single beam of light swinging back and forth, and a couple seconds later, a guard sauntered into view. He swung his flashlight from one display to the next, and passed the beam across the balcony of the second floor. His radio crackled, and he responded with something that I couldn't make out. Lisa and I shifted deeper into the bushes, and for the second time that night, I hoped Colin had the good sense to hide.

The guard's light swung across the bushes we were hiding behind, and my breath hitched. I thought he hadn't seen us, but then the light swung back and, this time, hovered on the imitation foliage. *Move on*, I thought, *just move on*. The light didn't move. It was pointed directly at us. The guard must've seen us, or part of us, or at least something that he felt needed to be checked out. The staccato footsteps drew nearer and nearer, each step making the light seem brighter and brighter. Finally, the footsteps stopped, and I thought he must have been standing directly on top of us. I was too terrified to look.

"Who's there?" It was an older guard this time, not the spiky-haired kid. I recognized the voice as the man who had given us a hard time about wanting to touch the dinosaur on that first day. Fisher, from my first vision. I risked a glimpse through the leaves and saw him standing just a few feet away, shining his flashlight in a wide arc. "Rookie, if you're messing around out here again, you won't be getting another warning."

The arc of his beam was nearing the dinosaur exhibit, and I thought for sure he'd spot us when suddenly a whirring, cranking, sputtering sound came from the metal ball contraption. Colin must've put a metal ball in the machine as a distraction, but now the guard definitely knew someone was here.

The guard turned and shone his light directly at the machine and cursed. He reached to his waist and pulled up his radio.

"Hey, Larry," he said.

"Yeah?" a crackly voice on the other end said.

The guard was about to speak again. I could see his mouth open, and I bet he even had the button on the side of his radio pressed. But before he could actually make a sound, something rushed out of the shadows behind him, something dark and lightning fast. It ploughed into the guard, knocking him to the ground. The radio slid across the linoleum, ricocheted off the coprolite exhibit and spun right into the dinosaur platform.

"Fisher?" the static-filled voice asked. "Fisher, say that again. We didn't hear you."

Grunts and shouts carried over from where the guard was now wrestling with the dark shadow.

"Hey!" This time the voice came from the balcony on the second floor, and a beam of light illuminated the guard and his attacker. "Fisher? Fisher, what's going on down there?"

There was a grunt, and then another voice yelled, "*Vite! N' avons pas le temps!*"

Two other dark figures suddenly rushed out of the shadows from farther down the atrium, sprinting toward the Buddha head. One of them had a stick of some kind, and the other was clutching a black sack.

"That was French," Lisa whispered. "He told them to hurry, that they don't have any time."

"French," I gasped. "Oh, God, we're too late!"

CHAPTER 36

"It's too early," Lisa said. "Isn't it?"

I glanced back over the bushes. The guard was pinned, and the man in black had taken the pistol from the guard's belt and now had it outstretched, pointing toward Fisher. The other dark figure was almost at the Buddha head. Just before he got there, two more flashlight beams came bounding down the far corridor, and the shadowy figure stopped and turned, scampering to the left. Two different guards rushed into the atrium, their guns drawn. They weren't close enough that I could make out their faces to tell if they were the ones from my vision but I imagined they were.

The man in black fired first. His shot echoed off the walls and rang inside my head like a church bell. The two guards ducked behind a display and fired back, splintering a bone on the T. rex's leg.

"What do we do?" Lisa asked frantically.

Suddenly another dark figure stood up on the right. Only this one I recognized. Colin. He held two long sticks that I quickly identified as Roman candles, each with the tip on fire. He pointed one at the guards and the other back at the T. rex and shouted a line from *Scarface*, one of his favorite movies.

"Say 'ello to my little friend!"

The ends of the Roman candles burst and colorful balls of fire streaked out, bouncing off people, displays, and the ceiling. The atrium filled with plumes of smoke. People were shouting and screaming. There was the sound of breaking glass and crunching wood.

The French man in front of us turned and aimed the pistol at Colin. Lisa went from trembling girl to ferocious animal in a split second. She screamed an ear-splitting shriek and pounced from our hiding place, landing on the man's back. Her hands were a blur as she scratched and punched. He shook right, then left, and finally managed to throw Lisa to the ground. As soon as she hit the floor, he turned, and pointed the gun at her.

This time I ran out of the bushes and jumped at his outstretched hand. I'm not sure if I kicked it or punched it, or maybe I just fell against it just the right way, but somehow I knocked the gun out of his hand and into the air. When it hit the linoleum, a shot exploded and a guard from down the atrium collapsed, grabbing his leg and screaming in pain.

The French guy looked bug-eyed in our direction. Lisa scrambled to her feet and held up her fists like she was ready to go another round. I took a step back, hoping that wasn't necessary.

The museum alarms burst to life, screeching for all the world to hear. The French man said something I couldn't quite hear but figured was probably a swear word, then sprinted out of the area, away from the Buddha head and away from the guards.

Colin's Roman candles suddenly extinguished. The vivid storm of colors fizzled out, and we were left in smoky silence. The two remaining thieves rushed down the atrium toward us. There was another shot and several shouts both in English and French.

"Stop where you are! Freeze! Don't move!" The voices seemed to come from all around and could be heard despite the wailing alarms. The two thieves dove behind displays barely ten meters from where we stood beneath the T. rex. A series of shots rang out, but I couldn't tell if they'd come from the thieves or the guards. Wisps of smoke hung in the air and made the whole scene look surreal. The looming T. rex only added to the feeling, as though we stood on a prehistoric beach during a thick fog.

A guard yelled, "Put your guns down, and come out. Now!"

There were more shouts and another series of shots. The fog thinned and I spotted Colin huddled with his hands beside his head. He made eye contact with me for a second. A look of desperation was clear in his wide eyes and unhinged jaw.

"We have to do something," Lisa whispered.

I looked around frantically. Colin still had his backpack so I had none of the things he'd brought, not that a block of cheese or a roll of tinfoil would be overly helpful at the moment.

It happened then. If Lisa hadn't been beside me—if she hadn't just spoken to me—I might have missed the sudden change in the color of her clothing and skin, but all at once the scene turned to shades of gray.

One of the thieves had leveled his weapons, and seemed to be taking careful aim across the atrium. I imagined the guards on the other side doing the same thing.

It wasn't 10:47, but for all I knew things had changed, our involvement might have sped things along. Either way, someone was going to die. Maybe several people. Panic surged in my chest like a crashing wave. I scrambled off the platform and grabbed the first thing I could think of—the coprolite—and heaved it as hard as I could at the thief with the gun. He must've seen me because he swung around just as the giant piece of dino-turd slammed into him.

His gun burst and a chuck of the T-Rex's leg, just to my left, exploded. The metal supports roared, and for a moment, it sounded like the bullet had woken the giant. Then something snapped, and a second later, more groans rose from the beast as the rest of the metal struts strained to keep the skeleton upright, but it was no use.

The guards and thieves must've heard the groaning metal, because all of them looked up as the skeleton lurched. Another groan, this one louder than all the rest, drowned out the museum alarms. It almost sounded like the dinosaur itself was roaring. A noise like a dozen cracking whips rose up all at once, and the T. rex dove to the floor.

The collapse of the dinosaur sounded like cannon-balls pounding the earth as hundreds of plaster shards scattered around the atrium. Something struck my shoulder and knocked me to the floor, then a chunk of bone—I think it was a rib—came out of nowhere and slammed into my stomach and knocked the wind out of me, sending stars swirling around my head.

Another gunshot rang out, followed by muffled groans, and the color flooded suddenly back into the room. *No!* I thought, not after everything we'd been through. I wanted to call out, but I couldn't manage a breath, let alone a shout.

Colin was suddenly beside me. He and Lisa heaved me to my feet and pulled me a few feet down the atrium before I slipped on a shard of glass or bone and hit the ground again, this time hauling Colin down with me.

"C'mon, guys," Lisa said. "We gotta get out of here.

The police will be here any minute." She helped us to our feet and pulled us toward the exit.

The three of us pushed against the glass door and bounced back. "It's locked," Colin said. The horror in his voice was palpable. Lisa rushed back to the atrium, grabbed a small wooden chair from a display near the doors, and held it over her head.

"We're already in trouble if we get caught," she said. "Another piece of glass isn't going to matter much more at this point." Colin and I backed up, and she heaved it at the glass. The chair hit its mark but bounced back and broke when it hit the floor. The glass didn't even crack.

Angry shouts echoed from the smoky haze and shadowy figures moved, some crouched, others upright, in all directions. It was only a matter of time before we would be caught. Colin dug into his bag, pulled out the firecrackers, lit them with the BBQ lighter, and threw them as hard as he could. The angry shouts became panicked when they went off, and I'm sure everyone in there thought they were being fired upon by a machine gun.

"We could hide in the loading dock," Lisa said, blinking at the wooden pieces at her feet.

"They'll find us," I said.

Colin heaved his backpack off the floor. "Stand back," he said. He swung the bag in three arcs and then released it at the window. The entire pane disintegrated, and the bag sailed through the door.

I gasped. "What's in there?"

"The head, of course," Colin said.

"You got it?" Lisa sounded awestruck.

Colin looked confused. "What? You think I was going to leave it behind after all that?"

CHAPTER 37

We sprinted across the street, through the gate of the playground, and dove to the grass. We quickly slipped off our dark clothes and shoved them back into our bags just as a police cruiser rounded the corner and pulled up in front of the building.

Lisa whispered, "Let's get out of here. Stay low."

"Wait. Look," Colin whispered, pointing to the roof. "Up there."

At first I thought it was just a shadow. But then a figure emerged. Two figures, both dressed in black. One of them was partially supporting the other as they moved to the edge of the roof. Then something slid across the gap to the roof of the bakery—a large plank by the looks of it—and the two thieves used it as a bridge to dart across, retracting their bridge on the other side.

"They made it out," Lisa said, with a smile. Then her face became serious again. "We can't wait around. No one's going to die, so let's get out of here. We have to get to the theater." She prodded me forward and then grabbed Colin's arm and pulled him too.

It was a bit early to say no one was going to die. Or that no one was dead. There had been a shot as we ran from the building, I remembered, and I knew for sure that one guard had been shot in the leg. Also, it wasn't yet 10:47, and for all I knew, Sok was still going to die along with the guard who got shot. Or maybe when the dinosaur collapsed, it had crushed someone. There were way too many possibilities and no time to think through them all.

We clamored over the fence and moved as quickly as we could through side streets and alleys, traveling the two and a half blocks to the theater. About halfway there, we heard more police cars, their sirens blaring as they raced toward the museum. There was a steady stream of people leaving the theater when we got there, and we shoved our way past and darted into the bathrooms to clean up.

It was 10:47 when I checked my watch. It was over, though I didn't have any idea if we'd saved anyone. For all I knew, we'd made it worse.

"You really got it?" I asked Colin as we washed the dirt and smoky smell from our skin.

He smiled and unzipped his bag and spoke with an English accent. "The name's Blane. Colin Blane. World famous cat burglar and super spy."

"Don't forget master wielder of Roman candles," I said.

He nodded. "That too." Then he said, "Don't worry, I know a good place to hide it."

"Are you sure?" Lisa asked.

"Trust me."

The relic seemed to smile as Colin pulled back the fabric, as if it had known everything was going to work out and it didn't have a worry in the world.

I didn't feel the same way.

CHAPTER 38

For the next few days, my body felt like... well, I guess it felt like it had been hit by a dinosaur. The *Gazette* didn't have an article on what had happened until Monday, but TV news stations from all over the country had picked up the story on Sunday and were interviewing all the guards who had been on the scene. The reports indicated there'd been a group of at least six thieves but none had been identified.

The spiky-haired rookie had been the one who got shot, but a full recovery was expected and he was being hailed as a hero. A couple others had minor injuries from bits of dinosaur shrapnel. Mr. Overton gave the museum's official statement, which was that there had been a break-in, and extensive, even catastrophic damage done to several of their artifacts. He listed several pieces, the T. rex skeleton, the Rube Goldberg machine, a few pieces of art, and of course, the Buddhist relic.

At first it sounded like he thought the relic had been destroyed, but then he added that the police were still investigating and that he couldn't comment further while the investigation was underway. I figured either they knew the relic had been stolen, or there'd been so much debris that they might have actually thought the relic had been obliterated by falling dino bones.

At the end of his statement, Mr. Overton took the opportunity to plug some of the new exhibits the museum would be displaying, and thanked the public for some of the very large donations that had come in to help cover repairs.

My mom said that she'd spoken to Mr. Overton, and despite everything, the museum had been given more attention this summer than ever before, and the public awareness it generated would be enough to keep crowds coming all year long. My mom said he couldn't have been happier.

Archer finally got back to us the Thursday after the incident. He asked us where we could meet and Colin insisted on the park near my house, which Archer agreed to. I thought he'd be furious with us for how things had played out, but he wasn't mad at all—quite the opposite, actually.

"Great job, guys," he said after we explained what had happened. "You not only saved lives, you made it so a life wouldn't be risked for the same purpose again. Well done."

"Then you're not disappointed that we basically robbed a museum?" Lisa asked.

"Greater good, Lisa," Archer added. "Property is meaningless compared to life. Frankly, I'm impressed. I know veteran members who wouldn't have had the guts you guys displayed." He patted her shoulder. "You saved lives, Lisa. Don't forget that. That's what matters." He rubbed his hands together and looked at us expectantly. "Did you bring it?"

"It's close," Colin said.

Archer nodded. "Good. I spoke to Sok and asked him to meet me here."

"You did?" Lisa asked. "Does he know we have the head?"

Archer shook his head. "I'm pretty sure he thinks I'm turning him in."

"Why would he think that?" I asked. "He could take us down with him pretty easily."

"Well, when I talked to him, I didn't mention you three. Thought it would be an interesting surprise." He smiled. "But listen, you guys did amazing. Feel good about it."

For the next few minutes that's exactly what we did. The three of us beamed. Colin's smile was wider than usual and I knew he was reliving the night in his mind and enjoying every second of it. Lisa, too, had a grin and seemed to relax. She leaned against a tree and nodded to herself.

About thirty minutes later, Sok showed up wearing regular street clothes, along with an elderly bald man who wasn't his grandfather but whom I recognized as one of the other monks, also in inconspicuous clothes.

Sok looked bruised and utterly defeated. He sighed when he got to us and said, "Okay. We're here. Let's get this over with." He looked around the area focusing on a few of the people wandering nearby. "Where are they?"

"Who?" I asked.

"What do you mean, who?" he asked. "The police, obviously."

"He really does think we're turning him in," Colin said. Then he laughed. "You think we'd get the police involved after what we did?"

"Then... what?" Sok asked. His eyes widened. "The head was destroyed... wasn't it? Didn't Overton say that? My grandfather is still at the museum hoping they'll at least get the fragments."

I felt a smile spread across my face and glanced at Lisa and Colin, both of whom had grins at least as wide as I imagined mine was.

Sok blinked and the old man beside him asked a question in a language that must've been Khmer because it sounded nothing like French.

"I'd like to show you something cool," Colin said. He led the way to the edge of a small creek that cut through the park, to a section near a huge oak tree. Then he nodded into the water, at a pile of large stones.

"I hope this wasn't disrespectful, but I was sure the cops were going to search our place. I had to stash it somewhere."

Sok stepped up and glanced into the water. I stepped up beside him and looked as well. At first I didn't see it. Then a fish swam by and paused right beside the submerged Buddha head, as if it were pointing it out.

Sok gasped. The old monk stepped up beside him and Sok said something in Khmer. The monk closed his eyes and said something and a tear rolled down his cheek.

He turned to Colin and said in English, "Thank you."

"I can't believe you guys did that," Sok said. "I mean, I just can't believe it."

Archer put his hand on the monk's shoulder and said, "I have some connections. It's going to take a few days, but I can get the relic back to Cambodia. It'll be safer if I do it. The police are going to be watching you guys."

Sok translated and the monk nodded and then said, "Thank you," again.

"I just can't believe you guys helped me with this," Sok said, shaking his head. "I don't know how to thank you for this."

"All in a day's work," Colin said, smirking.

Sok smiled. "If you're ever in London," he said, handing me a card with his email address, "I'd be happy to show you around."

When Sok and the older monk left, Archer turned to the three of us. "Very impressed, guys. Very impressed. I can't wait for you all to meet the members of our district."

Colin held out his fist and Archer smiled and bumped it with his.

"You did good, Colin," he said. "Very nice touch putting it in the creek. Very fitting."

"I'm nothing if not a showman," Colin said. He turned and glanced at me and Lisa. "Tell me this hasn't been the best summer we've ever had."

"In hindsight," Lisa said, "it's been pretty amazing."

"I'd agree with that," I said.

Archer gave us another nod and then unzipped his backpack, stepped into the creek and plucked the relic out and placed it into his bag. He zipped it closed and swung it onto his shoulder in a single movement. Then he turned and walked away casually, as if had a sandwich in his bag and not a priceless—stolen—artifact.

"That guy is so cool," Colin said as he watched him leave.

On Friday morning, I told my dad I wanted to go to therapy again. His eyes widened and he smiled. "I'm proud of you, son. I think you've come a really long way these last few weeks." We picked up Colin on the way. I had already explained Lisa's situation to him, so we stopped at her house, and the two of us knocked on the door.

"Hurry up, Lisa," Colin said, when she answered the door. "We have crazy-time with Dr. Mickelsen. Chop chop."

"You guys are going too?" Lisa asked.

"Of course we are," I said. "We gave it a lot of thought, actually, and if *you* need a bit more therapy, you can be sure that we need more too."

She hugged us both at the same time and looked like she was about to cry before she called back into her house that she had a ride.

My dad nattered on and on while we drove about how good it is for kids to get their feelings out, but then he slammed on his brakes when a man wearing torn clothes and sporting shaggy hair rode out into the street. I recognized him right away as the homeless man from the park. I gaped as he shook his fist at my dad and shouted incoherent curses at him for his careless driving. When he moved along, my dad blinked.

"Dean," he said carefully, "was that man riding your bike?"

The End

Learn how Dean's visions all started in...

THE DEAN CURSE CHRONICLES, BOOK 1

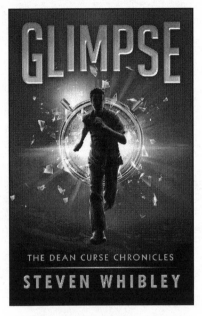

ISBN 978-0-9919208-0-8 / PB
ISBN 978-0-9919208-2-2 / HC

Dean Curse avoids attention the way his best friend Colin avoids common sense. Which is why he isn't happy about being Abbotsford's latest local hero – having saved the life of a stranger, he is now front page news. Dean's reason for avoiding the lime-light? Ever since his heroic act, he's been having terrifying visions of people dying and they're freaking him out so badly his psychologist father just might have him committed. Dean wants nothing more than to lay low and let life get back to normal.

But when Dean's visions start to come true, and people really start dying, he has to race against the clock – literally – to figure out what's happening. Is this power of premonition a curse? Or is Dean gifted with the ability to save people from horrible fates? The answer will be the difference between life and death.

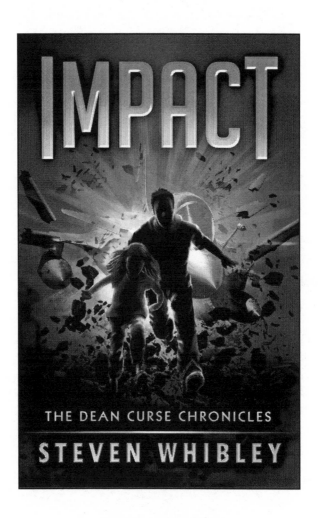

BOOK 3
Coming in 2013

ISBN 978-1-927905-00-5 / PB
ISBN 978-1-927905-01-2 / HC
ISBN 978-1-927905-02-9 / EBook

About the Author

Steven Whibley has lived in British Columbia, Alberta, and Japan; volunteered in Thailand, Myanmar, and Columbia; explored the ruins of Tikal, Angkor Wat, and Cappadocia; and swum with sharks in Belize. The only thing he loves more than traveling the globe and exploring new cultures is writing books (and spending time with his wife and two year old son, Isaiah, of course). Whibley is the seventh of nine children, and uncle to 30 nieces and nephews (and counting).